DOOMBREAKER

DIGBY HORLOCK

authorHOUSE®

AuthorHouse™ UK
1663 Liberty Drive
Bloomington, IN 47403 USA
www.authorhouse.co.uk
Phone: 0800.197.4150

Published by AuthorHouse 10/26/2018

ISBN: 978-1-5462-9969-1 (sc)
ISBN: 978-1-5462-9968-4 (e)

Library of Congress Control Number: 2018912529

Print information available on the last page.

© *Illustrations by Digby Horlock*

This book is printed on acid-free paper.

Dedicated to Ben, Issy, Jonny, Lottie and Phoebe

1

THE LAUNCH

"I've finished reading my book!" shouted Luke as he laid it down beside the bed. He was in the process of pulling the duvet over his head when Beth, having bounded up the stairs, ran into the room gasping, "What are you going to read next?"

Luke's voice, slightly muffled, rang out from under the duvet, "Someone told me there's a book about time-travelling back to ancient Rome and meeting and making friends with interesting people there".

"You've no idea how funny it is to hear a voice coming up from under a duvet, talking about friends in ancient Rome," Beth hooted.

"I'm Professor Absent Mind from Another Time," yelled Luke, emerging from under the duvet. "Tell me, madam, what are you doing here?"

"I've come to join the dance of time," she whispered, looking down at Kangaroo caringly and stroking him with her forefinger.

Kangaroo sat at the foot of the bed in the midst of a huddle of animals great and small, under the care of Luke Spencer. Luke liked to see the best in all things (except himself) whilst Beth, his sister, saw the best in Luke and was his closest friend and confidante.

They lived, most of the time, somewhere between their own imagination and the wind and trees and interesting things they found when they went out in the fields and forests running and dancing around playing.

"Bed!"

The call had come. It came two or three times, loud enough to carry up the stairs and register somewhere at the edge of Luke and Beth's playing.

"Shall we play the game?" asked Beth when all was quiet again.

"All right, Octopus is in charge and Big Ted is texting the others to pass on the orders".

"Octopus has his hands on everything!"

"Not everything, Squirrel is responsible for cleaning and tidying up".

Squirrel was unceremoniously placed in an upright position, overseeing what the other animals were doing. The gaze of her beady eyes slanted downward toward the floor because she could not be bent any other way.

Squirrel came into action when she was whisked up and, handheld, rushed here and there to pick up what lay on the floor. Each item collected was put back where it belonged.

Lying on the floor, Beth was looking up at the little cluster of animals on the bed when she came up with an idea: "Elephant goes to the back. He's going to keep the boat steady when they start to fish".

"Oh, and the diamond sword and diamond armour", added Luke, "Mouse can watch over that".

"Tiger can be in charge of her".

"No, Tiger needs to stay behind to defend the harbour", frowned Luke, "Leonard can come with us instead," he said, trying not to be complicated.

"All right, we'll put Leonard the Lion in the boat, he can be bodyguard". It was a rough and ready decision but Beth was comfortable with it. Anyway, it took too much effort to argue about it. After all, it was only for a night, when all was said and done.

"Is it time to go yet?"

Beth nodded and the two, who in some ways would think like adults, but still liked to play with teddy bears, climbed aboard to go fishing.

"We'll soon be through the waves", they sang. "We'll soon be through the waves, and into the world that no-one braves, and into the world that no-one braves.".

Then they closed their eyes, but Beth kept one open, because now the bunk beds had gone and she slept in another room, Luke was obliged to give the mattress an extra jerk on one side near the end of the singing, so she'd topple out. The pull came and she whispered, "Bye Luke", and slipped away.

"Goodnight", Luke called after her.

"And don't let the bedbugs bite," she shouted as she skipped back to her room, with Spotty Dog under her arm.

• • • • • • • • • ● • • • • • • • • • • •

The entrance to the tent was tied back to let the morning air flow into its stuffy interior. Luke lay fast asleep by the doorway. As the sun had been rising across the sky, the shadow protecting Luke from the sun's rays had moved too, and now full sunshine was bearing down on his face. A scorpion scampered across the hot sand a few centimetres from his head. Luke stirred with the noise and awoke with the hot sun beating down on his forehead.

Beth ran up with a cup of water and threw it across his face. Luke sprang up with shock and, instantly, had to shut his eyes tight against the sunlight's searing brightness. Sitting up, he said, "Where are you Beth?"

"Open your eyes and you will see".

"I can't, the sun's too bright".

"What can you hear?"

"Your voice, Beth".

"Can you hear anything else?"

"Are there some men talking somewhere nearby?"

"And some women, Luke," she answered. "Do you know who they are?"

"No, Beth, I don't".

"I thought they were with you". Beth's voice dropped, "They might be the only help we can get".

When Luke finally managed to open his eyes and peer over to see where they were, he could just about make out some people, some sitting on the ground, in hooded garments, and some wearing what looked like bath robes. They were all talking intently together.

While Luke was watching, they became calmer, as one in their midst rose up and began to teach. But Luke had more immediate things to think about. He looked back to Beth and asked, "Is there anything at all to drink?"

If Luke appeared to be in a daze, then Beth looked completely organised and efficient. Sporting a sun hat on her head, she swung a neat pack over her shoulder, unzipped a side pocket and pulled out a flask of cold water.

Bearing in mind what state Luke was in, Beth didn't even bother to pour the water into the cup because he'd probably drop it. She screwed off the top and handed the open flask to Luke. He took several long gulps then passed what was left back to Beth. The water would be all gone in a few moments, were it not for Beth's sensible planning. That was only her first defence against the desert. The pack was also a hydration system through which, every now and then, she sipped a trickle of water.

Luke's thirst quenched for the time being, he fired a question: "Where are we?"

Beth was at a loss how to answer the question because all she could recall was a superstore and a desert. Searching her memory, she retraced her steps.

"I was just going to sleep and about to choose my dream when a woman told me we were about to enter a desert. She was very kind and took me to the last shop before the desert. It was a huge store and it had everything you could imagine. It was so big, there were signposts in the store, one after the other, showing you the way to things you needed. I followed the sign for 'Survival Skills and Aids', then when I reached that section I found some shelves marked 'Surviving in the Desert'. I grabbed all I could but couldn't find anywhere to pay for things".

"So I asked some people and they said it was all right because it was all free. The next thing I know, I was in the middle of the desert, remembering that someone had told me there was a river and a road somewhere and that I had to find the way. Then I came upon you lying in the doorway of a tent with your arms all sprawled out on the sand below the guy ropes and your forehead coming out of the tent, about to burn in the hot sun".

"My head wasn't coming out of the tent. The sun was coming into the tent".

"Look the sun's been around since somewhere near the beginning of time, and it's massively bigger than you, Luke. It doesn't go round you. The whole world goes round it".

The effort of thinking about why they were here, was too much in the sweltering heat. Instead, Beth helped clean the dust off Luke, and started to get him organised. Behind them, the group of people moved away, making for the higher, empty-looking ground ahead. The buzz of activity had had died away.

As if for the first time, Luke and Beth became aware of silence. After a while, the air was so still they could hear their own hearts beating. That was eerie. Then, out of the corner of her eye, Beth noticed that the band of men had faded into the distance. She tugged at Luke's arm, "They've gone, we're going to be lost in the wilderness without them. Our only hope is to follow them, Luke!"

"OK," said Luke, coming to his senses. The wilderness looked so inhospitable, but Luke figured out that if those men and women were walking that way, then they must be going to somewhere where there is water and, if not then they would be returning.

Now fully awake, Luke jogged on ahead, with Beth behind continually calling after him, "Wait for me!"

It was so hot that after only a few minutes both were walking.

"It's just what you need on a hot day like this," boomed a voice.

Behind them was a man with a spool of cloth draped over his arm. They were not alone after all.

2

WILDERNESS

"Buy this and cool down," suggested the man with a spool of cloth. "It's just what you need in this heat," he said, with an appealing smile on his face.

Beth cut him short, "No, thank you," she said, eyeing the strips of cloth.

He stared at Beth and Luke for a second, then looked beyond them. What had caught his eye was the tiny, dark blur in the far distance that he thought might be some people. He stopped squinting against the sun to see what it was, because the fierce sunshine weakened and changed to a more subtle light. It was then that his face filled with interest and, without a word, he walked onwards as if he'd found something more important to do.

Luke slipped a thought to Beth. "Maybe he's seen a better market for his goods".

Left alone again and wondering what to do, Luke called a rest and looked for clues as to where they were. There was nothing to go on, but a suspicion was growing in his mind. Ever since he'd been awoken by the splash of cold water, he'd seen no evidence of the twenty first century, not so much as a backpack or a drinks can.

He watched the cloth seller striding on ahead, knowing that he was chasing the dozen or so people they'd been tracking. Should he and Beth really be following this crowd? The sky was wide open and the desert apparently endless.

Even without the mirages of the sun, Luke sensed something timeless about the tiny figures ahead, winding their way through the pristine wilderness. Not only were

Luke and Beth in another country, but he was beginning to wonder whether or not they were in another time too. Had time travel brought them here?

The haze was parting and the sun made everything appear to be merely some shade or another of white. Luke's forehead was soon damp with sweat, not least because he was worried that they might be lost forever, but he chose not to mention his misgivings to Beth, as he didn't want to upset her.

Beth had troubles of her own. She was anxious for another reason. The further they went into the desert, the more unlikely seemed the prospect that they would find the river and road she'd been told about, but even if they did, how would she know which way to go?

Keeping their thoughts to themselves, the two marched on, quickening their step. Within a few minutes, they overtook the cloth seller, who'd stopped to sort out his wares in readiness for a sale.

Progress was slow in the heat, but after ten more minutes, Beth and Luke had nearly caught up with the others, mainly because the band of people had stopped for a rest. As Beth and Luke drew closer, one of the men, who was leaning on a rock, turned and motioned to them to come near and join them.

It was the man everyone had been listening to before, when they were by the tent. He looked like someone they could trust. He was telling the others that he had seen Beth and Luke from afar as they'd toiled their way up the trail and even before, when they were at the door of the tent, he'd spotted them. With a friendly smile, he extended his arms towards them in welcome, hands angled elegantly downward ready to catch the hand of each.

Beth was the first to start running, when suddenly someone rose up, trying to bar the way. "What are you doing?" he snapped.

Beth felt as if she'd gate-crashed a serious discussion by a secret society on a day out, and immediately she stopped in her tracks.

Squatting on the ground, some looked up surprised or even shocked to see her, whilst some were clearly curious or bemused, but none had the twinkle of friendship in their eye.

"Let them by", beckoned the man who'd bid them welcome. "Come with me", he said gently, looking into their faces

Beth and Luke came either side of him, as if they'd known who he was all the while and, as he started to walk, they trundled along beside him. He looked back at the others. Some were reluctant at first, but one by one they fell into line and walked behind him along the way.

The trail was little more than a line of disturbed dust and stones, snaking upwards, near the brink of a bank of sand-strewn rubble that fell away to a wadi below.

A woman emerged from the little throng behind, and came up to walk with them.

She couldn't hide her bewilderment that the man was walking two children into the desert, yet there was a kindness in her eye as Beth caught sight of her face under the head covering.

Luke felt it was his place to say something, "It's hot, without a cloud in the sky," he said, rueing the fact that he sounded like a weather forecaster. "Would it be a good idea to find a cold cave to sit in?"

"And what would we do there?"

"Stay in the shade, I can't see man nor beast surviving out here in this hot sun", said Luke, cringing at the sound of the adult twang that had just come out of his mouth.

"The nosey hyrax lives in dark caves but he loves to sneak out into the sun," she informed him.

"Is that because he's nosey?" asked Beth.

"No, it's because he likes sunbathing!"

The idea of an animal with a big nose lying out on a rock to sunbathe in the wilderness, made Beth and Luke laugh.

The path, by now, was non-existent and the way ahead was covered over with a smooth layer of wind-blown dust and sand that had settled in the last hour or two. Beth looked back at the footprints they were leaving behind.

"You're making history," said the man.

Beth wrinkled her nose at the thought. She turned around again, to look back at her footsteps. "So," she said, "that was me a few moments ago".

"That was you, making your mark in the sand, and every one of your footsteps matters".

An indescribable sweetness tingled through Beth, at that thought. Not wanting to end the conversation there, she asked, "How do you mean?"

"What you did in the past helps to make you the person you are today".

"And what about now?" asked Luke.

"What you choose to do now may help you to be the person you can become".

"We have chosen to walk with you," said Beth, a little uncertainly. She still couldn't see where this walk in the wilderness was going.

"Knowing that you are walking with me now will make a difference".

She looked up and saw the smile in his eyes.

"I'm scared," whispered Beth, taking a step nearer to him.

"Why?" he whispered back.

"We're in the middle of nowhere and there's no-one here".

"I'm here".

"Why are you walking into the wilderness?" asked Luke, surprising himself with his own directness.

"The wilderness was like this in the past, it's wild and barren and empty now, and it'll be like that in the future," he said softly. "I like to be in a place that stays the same, where there's time to think about what's in the future".

Luke cleared his throat, "But isn't it rather harsh here?" He looked down at the grit and dust. "What can there be to learn here?"

"I come here to face the challenges of the wilderness to remind myself to stay the same, and to be ready to face every new challenge that comes to me when I leave the wilderness. What you learn here, is that life asks you questions and it's up to you to find the answers".

"How do we do that?"

"Keep your eyes and ears open. Listen to the wind and you will see what it does, and what it does will tell you where it comes from and when you know where it comes from you will make the right choice".

"We don't know what we're doing here, in the first place," said Beth, looking perplexed.

"Do you like puzzles?"

"Yes".

"When you're puzzled, you need to find the right clues that put you on track". Then he turned to the others and showed until they caught up with them. He started walking at the pace at which they kept step with him

Beth and Luke trudged along beside them, feeling the power of the sun beating down on them. Ahead lay a deep dip in the top of the bank, in which more sand than grit had been able to accumulate.

Luke looked down into the dip. Though it was dry, by the shape of it he could see it was a stream channel. But just as they stepped into it, a swathe of packed, dry sand came away suddenly from the bank, and slid as a detached carpet of sand which was breaking up, as it tumbled down to the bottom of the wadi.

In moments, their feet were taken from under them as sand poured downwards from all sides like sand in an hourglass. Down through the gap they were sliding, down in a sheet of moving sand.

Luke and Beth flew in the cloud of sand and dust, non-stop to the bottom, but the man who was with them managed to catch hold of a thin slab of rock that was being scoured out with sand flowing past it on both sides. It was about halfway down the slope. He held on precariously, suspended above the steep-sided wadi, while Beth and Luke were on the floor of the wadi, almost buried in sand.

When the sand slide eventually stopped, Beth and Luke looked up and saw him wiping the sand away from his eyes with his free hand, and shaking his sand-covered head. Sand sprayed in every direction outwards from his hair and beard. Catching sight of each other, they all burst into laughter, so much so, that he lost his grip on the smooth rock, slipped into the steep sand slope and, teetering forward, lost his balance and bounded down in huge leaps and jumps, his feet sinking and sliding into the sand one after another, like brakes that don't work.

Landing at the bottom, he sat up and they all exchanged glances – first of concern, then of relief. The man dug himself out and, leaving Beth and Luke to help each other out of the sand, he went in search of the backpack.

Beth's hydration system had separated from the pack and was hanging off her shoulder, with much of the tube buried in the sand. She pulled it out, wiped the mouthpiece and drew on it to see if it was still working. A dribble of sandy water rushed through the tube. Beth spluttered as it reached her mouth.

The man had returned with the backpack by now and he held out his hand in order to take hold of the system, which she passed on to him. He turned it upside down and poured out just enough water to flush out the sand, and he handed it back to her. Then Luke helped Beth to fit the hydration system back into the pack.

"Your friend who told us about the nosey hyrax didn't fall," said Beth.

"No," he replied, casting his eye up to the top of the ridge, "she is taking the women back the way we came".

Then, out of nowhere, he asked politely, "What is your question?"

Beth and Luke looked at each other blankly. They didn't know they had a question. In the quietness that followed, they both began to realize that perhaps they did have something on their hearts that needed saying. They knew they wanted to get somewhere yet they didn't know where, but it seemed impossible to turn it into a question. Before they could, the man spoke again.

"You want to ask me where you've come from".

The moment he said that it sounded ridiculous. Luke and Beth had often been stopped and asked the way to get somewhere, but no-one had ever stopped and asked to be told where they'd come from. Imagine if someone drew up in a car to ask you to tell them where they'd come from?

However, it was clear this was the question they wanted to ask. They had to admit to themselves that it was part of the reason they were feeling uneasy. Somewhere buried in the pit of their stomachs since they'd started the journey, was a tense feeling that they hadn't stopped to think about and which they'd pretended wasn't there. They couldn't put it into words exactly, so it hadn't been on the tips of their tongues. Now a stranger, who was becoming their friend, voiced the question for them. Where had they come from?

"Thanks for that", said Luke in a grown-up sort of way, as if things had fallen into place, even though they hadn't.

"You also have another question".

"You said we had a question, but that makes two".

The stranger smiled the moment Beth spoke, as if he understood her and admired her sharpness. Quietly, he leant his head to the side knowingly, with a smile, long enough for her to know that he was telling her she was going to need that sharpness. She felt at peace with that and asked, more calmly: "So what is the question we want to ask?"

"You want to know where you're going".

"That's true," admitted Luke. "We don't have a clue where we're going or how to get there".

"There are clues," he said. "I believe you will find your way, and when you have worked out what the clues mean, you will know where you are going".

Luke had a quizzical look on his face. There in front of them, was nothing but desert. He scratched his head. To find anything other than stones, sand and rock in this barren wilderness looked impossible. They were in the middle of a desert, covered in sand, without the slightest idea where they were or where they had come from or even where they were going. Their eyes met in bewilderment and just as they were reaching out a hand to each other, the only person who seemed to be able to help them was climbing back up the slope.

Luke shouted after him, "Where are you going?"

He was looking upwards to the men waving above him, but he looked down a second and called to Beth and Luke, "I'm going further into the wilderness with these men. Be sharp-witted. Help will come".

"You're not leaving us...," said Luke, climbing up toward him, but he was far ahead.

"You need to believe me".

"Are you coming back this way?" yelled Luke.

"No".

"Be seeing you again, I hope," he whimpered.

Luke waited for an answer but the man was out of earshot. Luke and Beth looked at each other for what seemed an age but it was probably only about two seconds. Then they heard some words faintly on the wind.

"Be see...doom storm...", was what Luke heard. Beth couldn't make out much more than a wind-muffled whisper, as she was further away. It wasn't much to go on.

He'd reached the top of the sandy bank and was standing in front of the little band of men, when they spotted him. He was talking to them, but he looked down at Luke and Beth for one last minute until he was sure they'd noticed him. Then he turned his head and pointed to the distance beyond them.

Try as they may, they couldn't get his attention after that. Beth swallowed, and looked hard at Luke for a long time, trying not to cry.

Luke put his arm around Beth's shoulder.

"Don't worry, Beth, remember the man has left us some clues".

"But he's a stranger," insisted Beth.

"I know what you mean. How can we trust him? But what matters now, is how to get out of this wilderness," grinned Luke. "I wish we hadn't come into the wilderness in the first place, but we had no choice".

"What do you mean, we had no choice?"

"The place where you found me in the tent was a deserted place. We were completely alone, except for those people. They were our only hope, and that's why we followed them into the wilderness".

Beth objected, "What about the cloth seller?"

"He was only interested in our money and we didn't have any".

"He must have known how to get out of the wilderness, though," said Beth, exasperated. She frowned, "All you had to do was ask".

"And that was all you had to do as well," stared Luke.

"We need to remember to ask more questions".

"If we can find someone to ask," said Luke, despairingly.

As they lay on their backs, considering their predicament, Luke and Beth failed to notice that the cloth seller they'd run away from, was standing high above, with a neat pile of cloths, tied up in an ox hide. He was looking disappointed. The men he'd hoped to sell to, after the women had refused his goods, simply filed past him along a narrow ledge that was taking them deeper into the desert.

"Let's get back to those clues," said Beth, trying to inject hope into the situation.

"We don't even know the stranger's name," said Luke, forlornly, "but I think I trust him. Do you?" asked Luke.

"I think I do".

"That's good, because his clues are all we have to go on".

FOOTSTEPS ON THE WAY

Luke and Beth fell silent as they looked around at the wilderness. There was no noise in the emptiness, except for the wind and an occasional shifting of sand in amongst the stones. Now and then draughts of air lifted a shallow dust cloud among the rocks. Everything looked dead. But life was there too, somewhere lurking in the caves and crevices or hiding under the sand, unseen.

As they sat, wondering what they were going to do, Beth drifted away into a daydream about a nosey hyrax staring up at the sky whilst sunbathing. She had no idea what a nosey hyrax looked like but she'd pictured a little animal with a big nose, wearing sunglasses, relaxing on a rock.

Luke touched her arm. "Come on, Beth, we need to move! We've only three or four hours of daylight left!" There was a note of desperation in his plea.

Beth tried being cheery to keep Luke's spirits up, as she hauled herself from the ground saying, "Back to the future!" with an old-fashioned voice. He looked unimpressed.

Looking back, she could already see some imprints of their footsteps. Nudging Luke, she pointed them out, "That's our history".

Luke shrugged. "Who's interested in history now? Let's think about the future. We need to make some choices here. Which way should we go?"

"That way", answered Beth, with a rather grandiose and welcoming gesture, and she waved her arm in the direction of a maze of rocky bluffs and dry, dusty wadis, stretching away to the horizon.

"That's not very encouraging", sighed Luke. "Is that the way the stranger pointed?"

"Yes".

"Then that's the way we go. It's the only chance we have".

Beth and Luke marched on with just that thought in mind. Keeping an eye on the place they'd left, they walked toward a little cliff that was in the right direction. Then doing the same from that cliff they walked to some rocks ahead, in the same direction. From landmark to landmark, they plodded on, keeping to the same trajectory. This took so much effort and concentration, that they ended up walking along like zombies, without speaking.

After half an hour, they reached a high point, and there, far in the distance, beyond a small range of hills, they could just make out a low plain, through the sun's haze.

Beth took heart. "You said that the stranger gave us some clues".

The wind was high and Luke couldn't catch what Beth was saying, so he came to a halt in order to listen.

"You said he'd given us some clues. What are they?"

"Oh, yes…now what was it?" Luke asked himself. He walked a step further, and stopped to think. "I know, it was 'bee see'".

"That's not much of a clue. There's no sea here and I haven't seen any bees," laughed Beth.

"That's only what it sounds like. We need to decode the clue".

"You said clues, not just one clue," said Beth, thinking she'd said that before.

"Yes, there was something else," remembered Luke, "It was about a storm. He said 'doom storm' or something like that".

"I hope we're not doomed to this wilderness," Beth rolled her eyes upwards, almost in despair. But, just as she did so, she caught sight of some people on top of a rocky rise not far away. "Look, Luke, there are people there!"

By the time Luke had looked up, the people were gone. "There's nothing there, Beth", said Luke. "You must be seeing things".

"No, I'm not," complained Beth. Again, at the side of the rise, she caught a glimpse of one or two of them. "Look! There!"

But they'd rounded the hill when Luke turned to see. "The sun must be getting to you, Beth. You're seeing mirages".

"Climb the hill with me. We'll see them from up there. They must be on the other side of the hill now".

Complaining all the way, Luke followed Beth to the top of the rise, but there was no-one to be seen. He lifted his hand in dismay, and gasped, "I told you, Beth. How will we ever get out of the wilderness if we keep wasting time and energy like this?"

While he was still speaking Luke spotted, about twenty yards away, the marks of fresh footsteps in a sandy patch, lying between the rocks. Luke had been in the wilderness long enough to realize that the raking wind could erase footprints within hours.

Luke didn't want to tell Beth what he'd seen, but he had to admit to himself that people had been on the hill only a matter minutes ago. He could almost smell their breath in the air.

Luke gulped down his pride, "You're right Beth". He pointed to the footprints, "I think they walked that way".

"Now you believe me," sighed Beth, hands on hips. "I know my eyes weren't deceiving me, they must be somewhere nearby".

"I haven't seen them yet. Seeing is believing," taunted Luke. "But I suppose it does look like they stopped here to discuss which way to go".

They both gazed at the footprints zigzagging across each other.

"Look over here, most of them went this way," observed Beth.

She darted off in a direction almost opposite to the one they'd been following, but Luke stayed where he was. He was more interested in a single set of footprints that peeled away from the others, in line with the way they'd been walking. "This set of footsteps here...," claimed Luke, waving Beth across, "go in the direction we're going".

"But, isn't it better to follow the way most people go?" objected Beth.

"Go on," urged Luke. "Convince me".

"It's bound to take us somewhere where people live," argued Beth. "Come on, it's like voting. You go the way most people's footsteps went".

"But, how can you trust them?" said Luke, testing her. "They could be bandits luring you into a trap".

"That's being paranoid".

Luke had to concede that Beth did have a point, "Perhaps I'm getting carried away, but it's not the direction the stranger showed us".

In that lonely place, Luke and Beth realised that they needed to think hard before making a move. It became clear they needed to reason out which way to go, very carefully.

"Give me two good reasons for going your way, then" asked Beth.

Luke clicked his fingers as if he'd had a brainwave.

"Listen," he speculated, "If someone goes off alone like that they'd have to be very sure of finding a place with water because there'd be no-one else to help them if they didn't".

"I'm still not sure," said Beth.

Luke shrugged, "OK, so what's going to decide it?"

The parting of the ways was there before them. It looked like there was everything to gain or everything to lose, or perhaps they would lose either way. Maybe they were going nowhere. Everything around them looked so vast. The sky was huge and empty. The barren hills were endless and the enticing plain was out of sight. Every moment, thirst itched a little more in their throats. They felt helpless and lost.

"We've forgotten where we've come from and we don't know where we're going," sighed Luke.

"Are you talking about us or the human race?"

"That sounds like you think we're not human?" Luke's half joke fell on deaf ears.

"It's not funny," she said. "Your question was making me wonder why we are here".

"Well, it's me who asked the question," owned Luke, "but, Beth, please don't get upset by it. I'm sure we'll be all right. It's just that a thought like that came to me when I sat on the sand looking at the waves, on a beach in Cornwall".

"Well, we're looking for the Bee Sea now," chirped Beth, now the lesson was finished.

"I think it's buzzed off," laughed Luke.

"Come on," said Beth. "There's no time to lose. A decision has to be made".

"Which choice do you think is best?" asked Luke, more warily.

Squashing her pride, Beth squeezed the words through her teeth as she trilled, "I think your reasons are right for following the single trail of footprints".

Luke dropped to his knees and touched one of the footprints. "Just because you're lost, you shouldn't follow any old person," he said.

"How do you know it's an old person?" asked Beth.

"I didn't mean an old person," said Luke, wondering if Beth was going to take literally everything he had to say today.

"That's what you said," she burst.

"What I meant is, why follow a person you do not know, a person who could be anyone?"

Reflecting on what he had just said, Beth suggested, "Yes, but that person must have a good reason for going off alone like that".

"Going downhill, like I said, you're bound to reach a stream or lake before long," said Luke, looking up with a smile. "That means water to drink!"

"Mmmm...water!" drawled Beth, longingly.

Luke sprung to his feet and surveyed the scene. "People don't live up here. If there are people around, they'll live down there in the valleys and that means, for us, that there's a chance of food and shelter too".

"The single footsteps then," said Beth, looking for Luke's agreement.

"Everything points that way," he winked.

Beth felt like hugging him. She herself was standing up, still with her hands on her hips. Her straggly hair had become matted with sand, a windblown mass of unruly curls.

They took a few steps downslope. The wind had picked up, so Luke stopped to lick his forefinger. He held it up to see which way the wind was blowing.

"The wind's blowing up from where we're going," he reported. "The wind always blows from cooler to hotter, so it should be cooler down there, where we're going".

"You mean we're going to where the wind's blowing from," said Beth. "That's so weird. The stranger we met, told us about an hour ago, that if we found where the wind was coming from, then we'd be able to make the right choice".

"Funny, that's what science says too," beamed Luke.

Feeling like a science detective, Beth asked, "Is it cool there because there's water down there?"

"I hope you're right. Perhaps that's where the 'bee sea' is," said Luke. All he could imagine, was a sea with rivers flowing into it and bees flying all over the place.

Beth felt like punching the air, but the reality of their situation kicked in as she reminded herself that they were still lost, their throats were parched and they were by themselves in the desert with little more than two hours of daylight remaining.

"Shall we have a drink from the flask?" she asked.

"There are only a few drops left," said Luke, declining it. He was trying to think on his feet. "And what was that other clue I said?"

"I think you said 'dust storm', it's very dusty round here"

"No it was 'doom storm'," remembered Luke.

"'Doom storm'," repeated Beth. She looked up at the thin, wispy lines of clouds in the sky. "But, there's not going to be any storm here tonight because the clouds aren't big enough".

"So the clue's not much use to us at the moment," concluded Luke.

"No, but don't give up, Luke. I'm sure you'll be on to it soon".

They ran down toward the nearest large rock. There they scanned the view to see if there was a way. Sure enough, down below were hints of a path twisting down between two towering, rocky ridges. As they walked into the hollow between them, the rocky towers loomed above them like the battlements of a castle.

"It's like a castle of doom," murmured Beth.

"No, it's not. We're going to find the way out," said Luke boldly, disguising his fear.

As they reached the hollow, neither of them wanted to mention the fact they'd noticed the path ahead simply disappeared. They both looked at the path petering out, in front of them, in the midst of swathes and tumbled sheets of dry stones,

Eventually, Luke muttered, "It's no good. We're clutching at straws".

"But I'm sure this is the way," said Beth, encouragingly.

"I don't just mean the path, Beth", said Luke, solemnly. "The clues are a bit airy fairy".

"But, they're all we've got",

"Yes, let's hope and pray something turns up to help us understand even one of them".

The farther down into the hollow they ventured, the more muddled and unsure they became. The air was still and the atmosphere ominous. Ahead, the slope was covered in grit and stones. Beth and Luke moved slowly, minute specks in the midst of a riot of rocks, inhospitable cliffs and crumbled stone, treading across dusty screes, with no idea of where they were going.

Not many minutes later, Beth and Luke came to a standstill. Looking around, speechless, they simply absorbed the silence.

There was nothing they could say.

After standing for a while like this, Beth felt a breath of wind on her arm. "Did you feel that, Luke?"

Luke shuddered, "Feel what?"

They clutched each other and held on tight. Luke spoke again, in a whisper, "What was it?"

Beth waited quietly for the wind. Luke whispered again," What was it you felt?"

"A coldness".

"You mean there was someone or something there?"

"No, it was a wind, a cool wind".

"I'm glad to hear that, and do you feel it now?"

"Yes... a little".

Luke looked straight ahead and down the slope, waiting. At first he imagined it, but after a while he too felt a draught of air.

"I felt it," he said, "but I wouldn't call it cool".

"Well, it's not hot".

"All right, I'll give you that".

The wind grew stronger, in fits and starts, until there was no doubt that a slightly cooler stream of air was funnelling its way up and into the hollow.

Trying to be scientific again, Luke suggested, "Let's walk down the slope with the wind blowing into our faces to where it's cooler and where there may be some water to drink".

"Yes," said Beth, enthusiastically. "Let's use the wind as our guide!"

To make sure they were going in the right direction, Luke licked his finger and held it up every now and then to find out where the wind was blowing from, "I don't know why I didn't do that before," he said.

Within a few minutes, a path could be traced going through a gap in the rocks. When Beth reached the gap, she yelled back, "There's a hidden lake!"

Luke rushed to join her and, sure enough, a lake faintly shimmered in the far distance, just visible through the heat haze.

Beth and Luke bounded through the gap, keeping away from some nearby cliffs, and picked their way down steep rubble-strewn slopes, searching for signs of the path. In among the ravines and bluffs below, they could make out a fortress, its roof tiles sparkling in the sun.

By now, they were running downhill at speed. Slipping on to their backsides they slid down gritty screes, braking just in time to thread their way through outcrops of rock lying about here and there.

Further down they could see the beginnings of a path halfway up the hill on the other side of a small valley. Speeding on, they clambered, hot and tired, up the hill to the start of the new path.

Although Luke and Beth felt exhausted and very thirsty, they ignored the fortress away to their left. They weren't sure they'd gain an entrance there and, anyway, they felt far too weary to go and investigate. The secrets of the fortress would have to wait. Peering down the path, they could see a wider track below them which turned sharply right at the foot of a line of cliffs.

"Would that be a safer route?" wondered Beth, out loud.

"It goes away to the side, it won't go down fast enough", was Luke's retort.

"Didn't you know that paths don't move so they can't go down fast?" quipped Beth. "They stand still".

"I suppose you think that's funny," wailed Luke. "I meant we want to go down as fast as possible to the lake".

Looking to see what their options were, Beth and Luke spotted a man on a rock where the path and track separated. As they strolled towards him, he looked familiar, sitting there in the late sun.

After some discussion, Luke and Beth decided they would turn off along the wider track. Wary of strangers, they tried to look as if they hadn't noticed the man on the rock, and they turned on to the road.

"You've come all this way for my goods", he called out.

'Oh, no, not him!' thought Beth. "It's the man selling scarves that wrap round your head", she whispered.

"I could do with one now, Beth," replied Luke, humbled by a hot day in the sun. "We don't have the money, but they're probably the best head covering we could have to protect us from the sun."

The cloth seller caught the last few words, "I only sell the best head coverings and I knew you'd need them before the end of the day, to keep the sun off.".

"They're not my kind of clothes", blurted Beth, to put him off before he could finish.

"But they're our kind of clothes, from Dan to Beersheba and far beyond. And what's more, you need them. Look I'll do you two of these.".

He held up a large piece of cloth then cradled it in his hands and lovingly rubbed the material between forefinger and thumb to show its quality. "It's a Simlah. Here, you wear it like this", he said, whisking it over his head.

"You don't understand. We're not here to buy clothes," said Luke. "We're here looking for somewhere, but we've only a couple of clues to help us find where we're going".

"We're looking for somewhere where there's water too", panted Beth, hoping the cloth seller would help.

"Wait a second, I might know where you can find water, but now that you know the name of this piece of cloth is a simlah", he said, stalling for time in hope of a sale. "Do you think it might be a good idea to know what my name is, before we do any business, that is?"

"I suppose so", said Luke, aware that there was little alternative.

"My name is Simeon and I sell the best clothes this side of Jerusalem".

"Jerusalem?" chimed Beth and Luke.

"Yes, Jerusalem is over there!" he said, flicking his thumb back over his shoulder. But Luke and Beth were transfixed as they looked beyond him.

Behind Simeon, they saw a man running straight for him with a dagger in hand. Somehow they found a sign language to tell Simeon without him turning round.

"Run down the track!" he shouted, and holding up the ox-hide of cloths and turning just in time, he absorbed the blow of the knife, and bowled his attacker over on to the ground. His attacker picked himself up and went scuttling off into the distance, without his knife. Simeon watched as he sprinted further and further down the path.

When Simeon had sorted out his oxhide and his wares, and found somewhere to put the dagger, he walked carefully down toward them. The shock of it all had brought them closer.

"Are you all right?" asked Beth.

"I'm not injured".

Apart from that, Beth had only one thing on her mind, "Do you know where we can find water?" she pleaded.

Simeon looked at the cliffs coated in the last, deep golden sunlight. He saw that the day was wearing on and the sun was about to set, and he looked at the two children in front of him, who didn't have the slightest idea where they were. Thinking he might live to regret it, he said, "Follow me and I'll show you where there's some water".

Greatly relieved by his offer, Beth asked, "Are we going to the big lake now?"

The cloth seller's face creased with a smile, "No, you won't be able to drink from that, it's too salty", and he walked off down the track.

Still shocked by the attack, Luke and Beth walked on nervously, a few paces behind him, whilst Simeon strode out boldly, his punctured ox-skin full of cut cloths, under his arm. Catching up with him, Luke asked, "Are you all right? Has that man gone?"

"He's half-crazed in the afternoon sun," replied Simeon. Then he thought about it, took a look at Luke, and continued.

"Listen, there are many Romans in En Gedi, not far from where I live and he thinks that because I'm not a Jew I'm a Roman sympathiser. It's all right, he's gone now".

"How do you know that?"

"Well, I know him. He's tried to hurt me before and then run away," said Simeon. "Neighbours in my village did warn me about him and they said that no-one else thinks like that around here. So they're on my side".

"Well, I'm sure if you pay attention to your neighbours, you'll be all right in the future," said Luke, speaking as if a man with experience, but feeling like a boy. Luke slipped back to talk to Beth, as Simeon marched on with head held high.

"Funny how things turn round when you're in need", whispered Beth to Luke as they walked along together. "To think we'd end up following the very cloth seller we were running away from!"

"And instead of selling us something, he protected us from harm," said Luke, staring down at the road. Then he looked up, cheerily, "We've found a road and someone is looking after us. That's good, isn't it?"

"Yes, I was told to look for a road," answered Beth. "and we've found one, if you can call it that. Now, we just need to find a river!"

"I'm so thirsty," said Luke, yearning for a drink as he gasped at the thought of a river full of cool, fresh water.

4

A NIGHT UNDER THE STARS

As they stepped over rocks and their feet crunched broken stones, there was a deep, hungry ache in Luke's stomach, a feeling of homesickness and lostness. They may be going somewhere, but where were they going?

Luke walked faster and Beth followed. Catching up with Simeon, Luke asked, "Where are we going?"

"You're coming with me, back to my village. No need to worry, my wife Salome will draw some water for you".

Beth was surprised, "Thank you, but why would you ask your wife to draw water for us?"

"Sssh," Luke gave Beth a look. "I think it's the custom here for a woman to draw water," he whispered.

"But we don't need a drawing of water".

"Beth, Simeon is not talking about getting a pencil to draw water".

"So what does he mean then?"

"I think he means that she will bring up some water from a well".

Simeon smiled politely, "Salome draws up the water for me. Otherwise, I would drink too much".

"Have you always lived here?" asked Luke, wondering how anyone could live in such a barren place.

"No, I come from the Thamud people to the south and Salome comes from Egypt".

"Are the people here friendly to you?" asked Beth bluntly.

Simeon, feeling under interrogation and wondering about the wisdom of inviting the two strays back to his house, took a deep breath and replied, "The Holy Scrolls say by their prophet Ezekiel, that even strangers like us can share the land of the Jews and bring our children up here".

"And do the Jews like you?"

"They call us by Jewish names, if that's what you mean. I don't know if they agree with my interpretation of their Holy Scrolls," Simeon was a bit larger than life, he took a different interpretation on everything. "But they like the goods we sell them," he laughed.

"Is it a long way to your house?" Luke asked, trying to take the conversation away from the danger zone, "I think my sister's getting tired".

"Tired? Would you like to ride a donkey?"

"But there's no donkey", squinted Beth, the sunlight streaming through the mountains into her face. "What was your real name?"

"My name is Shamim, and there *is* a donkey, little fiery one".

"What should we call you?"

"Call me Simeon, that's how I'm known in the village, and the donkey's just over there in a cleft in the rocks". Simeon pointed ahead to a narrow path that ran away from the main track, weaving its way across the scree toward a rock face.

The sun was slipping closer to the horizon as they turned off the trail and started climbing the rough ground toward a huge, detached rock as big as a small house. Beth trembled when she saw how steeply the ground fell away below the rock, but Luke spotted her uneasiness and held her hand all the way until there, behind the rock, they could see a small cave.

Inside the cave, the donkey was standing motionless, the remnants of a few sheaves of straw under her hooves. Beth felt better now. If the donkey had arrived there successfully by placing four hooves every time she moved, then Beth knew she'd be all right going back on her own two feet.

Simeon led the donkey out of the cave. "What's her name?" asked Beth.

"Donkeys don't have names. What are your names?"

"I thought you'd never ask," replied Beth cheekily. She was in a bit of a mood now she'd conquered the scree.

Simeon loaded the ox hide of simlahs under a strap and Beth enjoyed patting the donkey as she told Simeon what their names were. The rhythm of the donkey took her mind off how steep the slope was on the way back to the main trail. Back on track, Simeon helped Beth up, on to the donkey. Then he handed the lead to Luke, but Luke didn't know what to do with it.

"Walk with it, Luke", said Simeon.

"How?"

"You put one foot in front of the other and she will follow".

Luke didn't show it, but he was close to meltdown. "What if the donkey runs away?"

"A donkey which doesn't like the sun in its eyes and doesn't want to go anywhere very much, is not going to run away. Don't worry, let it take you back to the village, it knows the way better than you do," laughed Simeon.

Luke stumbled on to the track with donkey in tow, but feeling in tow to the donkey, until eventually they were moving along at a steady pace and his sister was bobbing up and down to the donkey's stride.

The thought that they were nearing a village made Beth feel safe after all that had happened. She was longing for a drink of cool water and the thought of getting one was good enough for now. Perhaps there'd be a wise person in the village too, someone who would understand the 'bee see' and 'doom storm' clues, who could tell them what they meant.

After about twenty minutes, Simeon stopped walking and called out something indecipherable in a high-pitched wail. A few seconds later, a woman came walking toward them. There was a short exchange between Simeon and the woman and then they both walked toward a well. She started to draw water from the well, and Simeon announced, "Salome, here are Luke and Beth. I found them lost in the wilderness".

"They must be thirsty," said Salome as she poured water into a pitcher.

"Let them have some now, then".

"Here you are". Salome beckoned and Beth and Luke came across and scooped up the water with both palms from the leather bucket that she'd pulled up on the end of a rope. Whilst Beth and Luke splashed as much water as they could into their mouths, Simeon leant over to Salome and whispered calmly, "That wild man attacked me with a dagger, just up the road from here".

An alarmed look spread over Salome's face, but, not to make a fuss of it, she looked downward and continued her chores. When Beth and Luke had drunk their fill, Salome cast the bucket down to the bottom of the well again, hauled it up full, then returned to filling the pitcher.

The sun was finally setting when Simeon and Salome invited Beth and Luke into their house. Inside were piles of cloth but otherwise it was rather bare. Salome brought out some hard-looking bread to eat, which Luke and Beth found very tough as they tried to tear away mouthfuls with their teeth.

"There's a man up in Jerusalem who says bread and life go together", said Simeon as he broke the bread into smaller pieces for them.

"What does he say?" asked Luke, trying to be polite as he stuffed his mouth with bits of bread.

"It's more what he did, Luke. He was speaking to a crowd out in the wilderness and there was hardly anything to eat, so he sat them down and gave every one of those thousands of people as much bread as they wanted".

"How could he do that?" asked Beth.

"It was a miracle".

"He's done it twice", said Salome. "It's not happened lately, though".

"Why?" asked Beth.

"I think it's because a number of people came more to eat the loaves than to listen".

"What's his name?" asked Luke.

"His name is Yeshua of Nazareth", said Salome, looking at Simeon to check if she should go on. Beth and Luke remembered hearing about a film called Jesus of Nazareth, but, apart from that, they didn't know much about him.

After a pause, Luke asked, "What is your original name, Salome?"

"You ask so many questions", said Simeon, beginning to tire of constant questioning, and looking to Salome, he signalled with his eyes that she need not answer. Luke thought to himself that perhaps it would be better to make conversation than to ask questions.

"No, it's all right", said Salome. "My name is Salma but you can call me Salome, everyone else does".

"That's an interesting story about the bread", said Luke, partly thinking it had something to do with the bread they'd been eating, "but it's a bit hard to believe, like this bread," and he laughed but no-one laughed with him. Luke gulped, realising he had not chosen the best way to say thank you to Simeon and Salome for their hospitality.

"I know you didn't like it because you never tried to belch," said Simeon.

Luke was confused, wondering whether family traditions at meal times were very different here. Perhaps they always told stories like the bread story, so he thought he would try it out, "We have stories like that about witches and magic where we come from".

"What we've told you is not just a story, it happened", said Simeon. "A friend of my cousin was there to see it".

"Impossible things happen with magic spells too," said Luke, seeming not to have heard what had been said. When no answer came from Simeon or Salome, Luke found himself studying the wood grain on the table.

Beth jumped in enthusiastically, "Are there any witches or wise men here who could help solve our riddle?"

"Perhaps we can", said Salome softly.

"What's the riddle?" asked Simeon, lowering his tone.

"It's four words." Luke whispered each word, as if he were engaged in espionage: "bee-sea-doom-storm".

"'Dughri', did you say?" asked Simeon, who was a little dull of hearing. But, before Luke could answer, Simeon began to explain. "'Dughri' means straight. Straight as a ruler, straight as a plumb line, anything less is not good enough for a carpenter or a builder who knows their trade. My Jewish friends tell me in the Hebrew Scroll of the Torah, the ten commandments are 'dughri', they are straight standards for living and.".

"Simeon, he didn't say 'dughri'," inserted Salome. "He said. 'bee-sea'".

As it was, Luke and Beth had not really been listening to Simeon's digression. They'd been looking at Simeon, because something had happened that he hadn't noticed, which left them holding their breath, struggling to smother laughter.

Puzzled at Beth and Luke's interest in magic and witches, Simeon had pulled away his simlah and scratched his brow, unaware that his hair had somehow been charmed upward by static electricity. His hair was now splaying outwards and upwards as if he'd had an electric shock.

"There've got to be standards!" thundered Simeon, trying to be credible but looking entirely ridiculous.

A furtive glance flashed between Beth and Luke. They could muffle a belly laugh no longer and together they burst into fits of laughter. In this moment of lightness, Salome saw her chance. She leant forward with an urgency in her eyes: "There is no life in it".

What she had to say came out of her heart, like a butterfly brushing your cheeks as it flew free from a locket that had just been opened. As they listened it was as if the butterfly were dancing, stopping to hover here and there, as gentle assurances punctuated Salome's words and her eyes shone in the flickering lamplight.

"Those who do witchcraft and cast spells dabble with the night," she said, as if to her own children. "The night is when you cannot see what you are doing. They are not with the light source, the Maker of life and the starry heavens".

"But I love the night. I love looking up at the stars", sighed Beth.

"So do I", agreed Salome, "but if we cannot learn from simple things, what can we ever learn? There are things we cannot see at night, even though the night sky is very beautiful. Water is beautiful, I love looking at the ripples of sand through the clear water, but if I stay under the water I will drown".

"You're making me scared of water and night now," said Luke, starting to frown.

"We need a normal awareness of things in order to stay alive," replied Salome. "If you run fast and don't look where you're going, you'll trip and hurt yourself. It's just the way things are".

"I guess you're right".

"She is right, Luke. You're always running and banging into things because you get too excited and don't look where you're going," Beth, not immune to fear herself, turned to Salome and said, "you've scared me about swimming in the big lake at the bottom of the slope and I was so looking forward to it".

"No need to worry there," said Salome reassuringly. "If you swim in the big lake you can't sink because it's full of salt. We call it the Sea of Salt."

"Let's talk about the stars," said Simeon, having brushed his hair down.

"I like looking at stars," said Luke. "I want to learn all about the universe. There are millions of stars that you can't see with the naked eye".

"How do you know that?" asked Salome.

"Because there are telescopes that show them to us, and they prove that the universe is getting bigger all the time".

"That sounds like Simeon," laughed Salome.

"Yes, I eat too much and I'm getting bigger all the time," he said, slapping his stomach. "But, tell me," yawned Simeon, "where can I find these telescopes?"

"He only wants to sell them," said Salome. She looked across to Simeon, but his eyes were closing and he was beginning to breathe heavily.

"Where are we going to sleep?" whispered Luke to Beth. Beth tried to round off the conversation and find out.

"Well, we've talked about all sorts of interesting things," she said.

"What have you learned from tonight, then?" asked Salome.

"I've learned, for example," said Luke, rather formally, "that food is good when we put a little salt on it, but bad if we put too much salt on it".

Beth's heart sank. Luke may have been tired, but he clearly hadn't been listening. Yet Salome saw something in it.

"So now you understand," she said. "It's what you do that makes the difference. The night is wonderful, but you need to carry a light if you want to see where you're going!"

Simeon, stirring again, but only half-listening, heard the word 'light' and took it as a hint to go and start another lamp.

"What you're talking about, where we come from, is called 'common sense'," said Luke.

"Yes, but Luke doesn't have any," teased Beth.

Simeon, by now, had lit the lamp, having filled it with fresh oil. The flame flickered to life and he called out to Luke and Beth, "Come on you two, it's time for bed. Take some of those cloths from the corner there".

They followed his steps up on to the roof.

"How are we going to sleep on a roof?" asked Beth, expecting an answer, only to find that they were being dumped on to it without an explanation. When Simeon's silhouette, backlit by the lamplight, passed down below roof level, Beth and Luke looked at each other, aghast.

"This must be the way they do things round here," sighed Beth.

"They have a good chat with you then throw you on the roof!"

"What do they do with their enemies?" she wondered.

"I don't think those two have any enemies," said Luke. "Anyway, it's nice and cool up here".

"What are you talking about, Luke? Simeon was attacked by a man with a dagger today!"

"Oh yes, I'd forgotten about that. Simeon's hair was so funny, though".

"He looked like he'd seen a ghost!" They laughed helplessly until the thought of ghosts seemed a bit frightening in the darkness. Luke decided to speak quietly in case there was anyone around. "We still need to make sense of the clues we've got," he whispered.

"Simeon never said what 'bee-sea-doom-storm' means, did he?" whimpered Beth.

"He probably doesn't know, but it was good to listen to Salome".

"I like Salome".

"So do I," admitted Luke, "and I like Simeon too, he's been very kind to us".

"Yes".

Luke and Beth felt thankful as they covered themselves with pieces of cloth. Up above, the sky shone with thousands of stars. Luke showed Beth the spread of the Milky Way and the shapes made by the star formations they could see.

Luke wished he could tie all his cloths together, because they kept falling off him. After fiddling around with them for some time, he looked up at the stars, and wondered where they'd be going the next day.

"This journey... it's going to take some working out," he said.

Beth had noticed a belt of stars, high in the sky, seeming to make a pattern. "If we find what the clues have to tell us," she said, "it'll tie everything together in a pattern, and we'll be able to make sense of it all".

Luke pointed, "That's Orion's Belt".

"If we have as little food as we did tonight, you'll need a belt to stop your trousers falling down, Luke," joked Beth.

"I could do with a belt to keep all these cloths on top of me!"

"Simeon and Salome are trying to look after us...," said Beth, beginning to snooze, "but they've never heard of duvets". And, with that, Beth fell asleep.

Luke looked at her sleeping for a few seconds. Thinking about how much care Salome and Simeon had taken of them, he felt grateful that they were now somewhere safe after getting lost in the wilderness. Then he fell asleep.

Beth woke for a moment, blinking and wondering where she was. When she saw Luke lying quietly next to her on the roof making no sound other than breathing, she fell back to sleep. They weren't to know that they would be staying with Simeon and Salome for over a week, but if they had known, they would have been very happy about it.

5

THE DOOMSTONE

"I must go up to Jerusalem," said Simeon dramatically, "I'm selling nothing here. We're the first to get wares from the south, Salome, so I should go up to Jerusalem and sell them there before the other traders arrive".

"But they're just the same things all the time, aren't they?" said Salome, trying to make sure he was thinking straight.

"No, there are new goods like incense and silk coming through En Gedi now".

"So you'll be taking more than the cloths?"

"I've found some new contacts and I'm taking anything that's new now: spices, pots, everything. I've just received new supplies from the desert traders. If I arrive first, people will want to buy from me at a good price".

"So you need to go immediately", said Salome, trying to be sensible about it.

"Yes, but I have to wait for Luke and Beth," insisted Simeon, even though he was aching to go.

"Why?"

"Because I promised I'd take them up to Jerusalem"

"Do you want me to pack some bread and raisins for you?"

"And a small wineskin full of water". As he always did, Simeon pictured in his mind the way he should go. This time he'd need more water as there'd be three people which also meant more weight on the donkey with one of them riding on top all the way. Usually he risked travelling the most direct way over rough ground to start with, and he would carry a small skin of water that lasted until he arrived in Jerusalem. But this time, he planned to take them to the north end of the Sea of Salt first and take on fresh water above Jericho, without going into the city.

Inwardly, Simeon was always excited about going up to the bazaar at Jerusalem from the almost deserted place they lived in, but he never dreamt of letting anyone know that, and always acted as if it was just a job he had to do.

In order for his visit to be a success, Simeon needed to remember many things. Fortunately, he had Salome to do much of the remembering. She was like a mother hen, making sure everything was packed and ready for Simeon to strap on to the donkey, and this time with Beth on top.

· · · · · · · · · · ● · · · · · · · · · · ·

Beth and Luke were scuttling up ribs of rock and dusty slopes that rose behind the village. Climbing quickly upwards, Luke dislodged a stone. It wobbled, then started to roll down. He called behind him, "Mind out, stone coming!"

The stone unnerved Beth as it flew past her at high speed.

"Can't you be more careful and think about who's below you?" she shouted.

Luke was too pre-occupied to answer. "Look, over there, can you see the caves?" he yelled.

Up to the right, there were holes in the cliff in completely inaccessible places. Beth took one blink up there and shouted, "No! Please don't go up there! The slope's steep enough here Luke".

"It's not as steep as the slope by the cave where the donkey was, and you managed that".

"I'm stopping here".

Luke skidded down the gritty slope to where she was.

"Come on!" he said. "Grab hold of me and we'll get to the bottom of the cliff together".

"Only that far, though, no further!"

Luke half encouraged and half dragged Beth upwards.

She shrugged, "Leave me alone!" and pushed him away.

Although the ground wasn't as steep as it was below the cave where the donkey was skulking the day they came, it was still steep enough for Beth to be near the limit of what she could endure.

She decided to warn Luke, "I'm only going up to the foot of the cliffs. I'll wait there for you while you go and explore".

There were two cliffs above, separated by a steep gully, which caught Luke's eye. "Let's go up this gully. There's a cave on the side-wall just above".

"I won't be able to climb up there".

"OK, let's sit at the bottom of the cliffs," suggested Luke. "I've got something to tell you anyway".

"You're thinking we're in another time," said Beth, pre-empting what he was going to say.

"How did you know that?"

"Because I know you, Luke," she winked. "You've been a bit weird lately. I can tell you've been away in your head somewhere, and, well, I thought about it too".

"But how would you know we're in another time?"

"Because what else could it be? How else could we possibly be talking to people who don't know what a telescope is?"

Luke was looking high above. "We'll talk about it later. I need to climb up there," he said.

"Please be careful," begged Beth. "I'll wait for you here".

Luke scrambled up to a place just below the mouth of a cave. He looked back at Beth, then stepped from the scree on to a foothold on the side-wall. As he lifted his other foot to another hold, the first foothold broke away from the cliff and he tumbled about ten feet down the gully on to a dusty ledge just above Beth. Feeling a flicker of pain, he stood up and brushed the dust off his clothes, as if nothing had happened. He found himself standing on a ledge that was level with Beth's shoulder.

"Nice to meet you, do you come here often?" asked Beth, with a cheeky grin.

"Oh, just slipped out to see someone," he chirped.

"Slipped down, more like", laughed Beth.

Luke allowed himself a polite laugh at his own antics, and hoped to put an end to the episode with a workmanlike clap of his hands, to shake away the dust.

"Sssh, listen, something moved…over there," said Beth. "Could it be a nosey hyrax?"

Luke was captivated by the possibility. Inquisitively, he shuffled further along the ledge, out of sight. After a few seconds, he shouted back to Beth, "There's a cave here! Come on!"

Beth clattered along the top of the scree below the ledge.

Luke called to her again, "I'll pull you up," which he did, almost splitting his trousers in the process.

In front of them, Beth saw a large stone leaning against the entrance to another cave. It was almost as high as Luke and appeared to have been rolled in front of the cave, leaving only a small gap, just big enough for Beth and Luke to crawl through. Partly through fear of something or someone being there and partly just to hear the echo, Beth shouted: "Hello!" The sound resonated. She shouted even louder, "Hello!" and they both heard a faint echo.

Luke knelt down to look, his forehead pressing against the angle of the rock above the gap. As he moved away, he saw the light return to a corner of the cave. Beth squeezed herself through the gap, and shouted, "Is there anyone there?" As the echo rang around the cave, a flash of light shone up from the floor and Beth ran toward it.

· · · · · · · · · ● · · · · · · · · · · ·

"They can't be far," said Salome.

"Unless they're back soon," said Simeon, without much hope, "I will be going without them".

"But they won't know what to do without you," said Salome, her eyes searching his. "You're the only help they've got to solve the riddle of the clues!"

"All right, if you put it like that". Simeon had spent many hours trying to solve the riddle, and now he was determined to find a wise person in Jerusalem who might be able to decipher what the clues meant.

"Wait for them," said Salome, knowing Simeon would be disappointed if he left without Beth and Luke. "You know where you're going, you'll get there soon enough", she said, reassuringly. "They only went up to the foot of the cliffs to play".

Glancing up there, the cliffs looked gaunt and uncompromising. They seemed immovable obstacles like the things that were stopping him going to Jerusalem. Then he remembered Luke and Beth sliding and playing on the scree the first time he took them there.

Salome saw him smile to himself, "What are you thinking about, Simeon?"

"Life does ask me questions," he said. "Sometimes it makes me wonder about where we're going and what we're doing," he sighed.

"We've just got to get the money we need to keep a home and we'll be all right," came Salome's simple answer, which made him feel he ought to be on his way. Why couldn't they just live in Jerusalem, then he wouldn't need to keep making the journey.

"What are we doing here in this little place? Hardly anyone lives here and all I do is receive goods and sell them on. Life's got to be more than that?" Simeon's tone was verging on melodrama.

"Life's about our love for each another", said Salome, soothingly. The lack of trade hereabouts, even the prospect of a violent anti-Roman chasing after him, paled into insignificance when he looked into her eyes. "You're right to wonder," she continued. "We can't make life all about money, we'd just end up getting more and more selfish that way".

"What, me get more selfish?" bayed Simeon indignantly. He hadn't realised that Salome was listening to him, considering him, not accusing him.

"I'm not just talking about you," said Salome, correcting him. "I mean me, you and anyone else who puts money in the centre of their life. You can become selfish and unkind".

"Like that tax collector in Jericho".

"What about the tax collector in Jericho?" asked Salome.

"Didn't I tell you about him? Last time I went through Jericho, everyone was talking about him".

"You mean he was very selfish and charged too much tax so he could hold back lots of money for himself," said Salome, remembering what tax collectors could be like.

"No, he stopped being like that and gave half his money to the poor and began to pay back the people four times the amount he'd cheated from them. Honestly that's what he did!"

"What would make him do a thing like that?"

"He met Yeshua, who forgave him for all his dodgy deals".

"Do you do dodgy deals, Simeon?"

"No, I just try to make a profit!"

Just then, Salome and Simeon heard Beth and Luke's voices as they came running down to the house, throwing themselves through the door in a wave of excitement.

"We discovered a cave up on a ledge in the cliffs with a great big stone across the entrance", said Luke, breathlessly. Beth could hardly contain herself, as her suspicions burst out of her mouth, that there was hidden treasure there or that maybe it was a magician's hideout.

Simeon turned round and looked at them sternly, "That's the Stone of Doom", and the way he said it took the wind out of them.

"And we found this," said Beth, holding out a coin.

Simeon took hold of the coin, then flipped it over and said, "That's Emperor Tiberius on the back. I'll be earning some of these coins up in Jerusalem."

"There you are, Beth!" cried Luke. "If Simeon is using this coin as currency then we must have gone back about two thousand years in time!" Such a conclusion was lost on Simeon and Salome, but they could tell Luke was excited. But Beth had gone further. She had unravelled a mystery.

"That's one thing, Luke," said Beth, calming him down. "But what's more important for us now is that we've found one of the clues. It wasn't 'doom storm' that we heard in the desert. It must have been 'doom stone'".

Before Beth could say another word, Simeon, who had been trying so hard to interpret the clue for them, raised an eyebrow: "So that was what your friend was trying to tell you," he grinned, "to find out how to escape being trapped".

Were they trapped in time? To Beth and Luke, it all seemed as brutally clear as the outlines of the cliffs and as sharply focussed as the raw heaps of stones behind Simeon's head.

"If I didn't know better," said Simeon, "I'd say your friend knew that you'd come here and that you'd find the Stone of Doom".

It was a shattering thought. Everyone was stunned into silence. After a minute or two, Beth and Luke attempted to piece it all together.

"It does fit our 'doom stone' clue," said Luke.

"What are the chances of that?" asked Beth.

"Doom means you don't have any chances at all," said Simeon, slightly misunderstanding the question.

"The doom stone is nothing to be afraid of," said Luke, calmly, "it's only a big rock standing in the way, just a quirk of nature".

"Yeah, a big rock must have fallen on to the ledge from the cliff thousands of years ago. It's a pure accident that it's there," agreed Beth.

"For that big stone to fall from above and land so that it completely covers the cave entrance - that would be a chance in a million, wouldn't it?" said Simeon.

"I suppose so," Luke conceded, "but, it doesn't completely cover the cave entrance".

"And that's exactly why anyone who enters might not have a chance," boomed Simeon. "The gap is inviting, but no-one ever goes in there," Simeon's lower lip quivered slightly. "You see, if anyone intended you harm they could close the entrance while you are still in the cave, you would never get out".

"So that's why it's called the Stone of Doom," said Luke, the truth dawning on him, "because someone could push the stone across the entrance while you're in there and there'd be no way of escape".

Beth looked puzzled. "But what does that have to do with doom?" She'd already pictured doom as something to do with spells that could not be broken.

Simeon looked darkly toward the cliff, weighing up what he had to say next.

"We live in a small village and people can't help bumping into each other. This is how it's been in our village for hundreds of years. Let's say you lived here long ago and you accidentally upset someone by leaving the well dirty or your goat churned up the ground outside their house.

There might be little else to talk about and small things can become big things and all this is whispered behind doors so then dislike grows and dislike can grow into hatred and, yet, even though it's only a small village, you wouldn't know who your enemy is. If you went up to the cave one day, you wouldn't know who might want to follow you there and see you going into the cave on the ledge and then come up and close the entrance and trap you forever".

"When you realise this could happen, after a while you get suspicious and other people are suspicious because they're not sure who their enemies are either. Then, something else happens – the fear and suspicion turn into superstition. A mother and father tell their child not to go into that cave for good reasons, because they want them to be safe, but, to make sure they do what they're told, they tell a scary story to make the point. They say there's a fiend up there who traps you in a cave if you go near the cliffs and you'll never get out. They say this partly because they don't want to be bothered watching out for their children and this does the trick, scaring the children away from the cliffs altogether. After generations, the story becomes folklore. The folklore makes the stone a sinister object to people. They call it the Stone of Doom and now no-one goes near it".

"People associate it with the fortress of Hyrcania, the one you saw when you came down from the wilderness," Salome looked up at Simeon as if they were remembering something together, and there was sadness in her eyes. "When we were children, King Herod threw his enemies in there and killed them. They say he even killed little babies. Hyrcania was a place of doom".

Salome nodded toward the cliff, "So that's why everyone's afraid to go there. You were both brave to go in".

Beth shrugged, "We didn't have a clue what we were doing".

"The good thing is you've helped us to begin to understand the clue that our friend in the desert gave us," smiled Luke.

"How does a doom stone help us, Luke?" asked Beth, testily.

"Let's not jump to any conclusions," said Luke. "We need to learn something from it, but I don't know what it is yet".

Simeon raised his eyebrows in agreement. "We all still have things to learn. Salome and I have just been talking about what we're learning from life".

Instantly, Beth secretly wanted to go to classes and efficiently tap neat notes of lessons learnt from life into her tablet, and file them away. But somehow she sensed that only out in the big, wide world would those lessons be of any value.

Boldly she asked, "What have you learned from life, Simeon?"

"Don't get him talking," groaned Salome, as Simeon scratched his head. "You need to go and get yourselves ready. We're going to Jerusalem!"

"We?" asked Simeon, a little perplexed.

"Yes, I'm coming too. I've never been to Jerusalem".

"But, where are we going to stay?"

"You never thought about that, did you? What were you going to do with Beth and Luke?"

"I suppose I hadn't thought about it really".

"Don't tell me, you were going to go and sleep with your wares with the donkey tied up next to you, and just let Luke and Beth roam the streets, because you didn't think about it".

"So, what would you have done about it, Salome?"

"Well, when we get to the bazaar, I'm going to ask Sara if she could put us up for a week. That should give you time to think".

"I'm glad you're coming, Salome, then we can both look after the children," said Simeon.

"Children?" Luke was outraged, feeling more grown-up than that. "Did you know that we can teach you things that you've never heard of?"

"How can that be?"

"We come from the twenty first century of the Common Era".

"What's the Common Era?"

"It's from when we first started counting time forwards".

"So you're saying we count time backwards?"

"I think that might be true".

"I don't think so, Luke. The Romans have been counting time forwards for nearly eight hundred years, since the day the city of Rome began".

6

THE HEAVENS ARE TROUBLED

"We're going to Jerusalem now. It's a long walk, so no going out to play before we set off," warned Simeon.

"All right," agreed Beth, "but we walked a long way to get here, so we should be able to manage a long walk".

"I'm talking about being on time," scoffed Simeon.

"We've come a long distance in time too," said Luke.

Instantly puzzled by that, Salome asked, "How can you say that time is a long distance away?" That Beth and Luke were from some distant time in the future was still incomprehensible to Salome and Simeon.

Simeon raised his hands in the air, palms open, "The seers and soothsayers never told us anything like that!" he declared.

"You know," said Salome, more calmly, "We can't understand why or how you came here, but there are people among us that seek to understand signs who might understand".

"Perhaps our clues are really signs," said Luke, aside to Beth.

"I think signs are something you read from what is happening around you, Luke," she whispered.

"How would we know if something was a sign?" asked Luke.

"You mustn't jump at the first thing you see," cautioned Salome, "but it should be obvious. We remember some wise men who saw something out of the ordinary and realised it was a sign," said Salome. "They were three astrologers who followed a bright star that shone a light on a little child King".

"And did they find him?" asked Luke.

"Yes".

Luke's eyes brightened, "Perhaps there are wise men like that in Jerusalem who can find the exact place to go to find a time turner"

"No-one's ever heard of a time turner around here," wailed Simeon, lifting both arms in another gesture of disbelief.

"So the child King was baby Yeshua," gathered Beth, "but wasn't there a king already?"

Salome tilted her head to one side, wistfully, and sighed, as a tear rolled down her cheek, "The King Herod of those days heard the child King was born around Bethlehem but didn't know which child he was, so he had all the little children around Bethlehem murdered".

The room was quiet and Beth and Luke could sense the sadness of the past. Finding it impossible to imagine any twenty first century government deliberately targeting little children, Luke was left in no doubt that he had come from a different world.

"Wait a minute", he said. "Isn't this the play we had at Christmas? Three kings following a star and finding baby Jesus?"

Unable to answer his question, Simeon went on, "There are people in Jerusalem who seek signs of the future. They might tell you something about signs that are for your times, but we need to start our journey there soon".

Simeon's heavy hint was enough to get the other three loading up, until finally, Beth clambered on to the donkey and they started to make their way out of the shadows into the sunlight.

Passing the well, by the way they had entered the village, Beth wondered whether she would ever see it again, or whether she might ever again chase Luke up the stony slopes above.

"So, Luke, Yeshua is the baby Jesus," she said, waggling side to side, on top of a moving donkey.

"That's it. He would be older now. We must be here in BCE, in what they used to call BC".

"Didn't that end when Yeshua was born?"

"No, I think it ended when he died, because the Common Era used to be called AD, which I think means 'After Death'".

"No, it doesn't'".

"What do the letters stand for, then?" asked Luke, blankly.

Beth replied, "I think they mean after he was born, in Latin".

As they slowly picked their way down toward the Sea of Salt, Luke and Beth started to appreciate how large it was, as it spread out before them in both directions. Simeon, fully at home with where he was, stepped up on a rock to point out the way along a track.

It was several miles before they stopped for their first rest.

Beth stepped down from the donkey, taking care not to knock the ox hides of goods and belongings on to the ground. Luke joined her and they walked along together. The Salt Sea sparkled and danced with reflected sunlight. Near to land the water was almost fluorescent as it lapped the shore. The shallower water shone a brilliant turquoise in the baking sun. Imagining it to be cool and refreshing, Beth and Luke ran down toward the water's edge.

Like long combs of fossilized wool drooping down to points, crystallized salt stalactites hung down in front of them. They hung from a huge boulder covered in white rock salt. The ground was covered with knotty, white pillow-shaped salt deposits. They were difficult to walk over, so Luke gave up and turned round before reaching the sea. Beth reluctantly turned back too and followed him. Just as well because, with a long journey ahead of them, Simeon and Salome didn't want to stand around too long.

"I wish I could have jumped in and splashed in that cool water," squealed Beth.

"In summer, you can get very hot there," said Simeon, "but any time of year, it's hard to stay under the water in the Sea of Salt. You'd float on the surface and get burnt in the sun today".

Luke laughed, "You'd be toast, Beth." Beth immediately felt a longing for buttered toast back home in the twenty-first century.

The heat of day was still rising and it wasn't long before Salome issued a warning, "We'll need to stay in the shade as much as we can".

"Will we get sunburns?" asked Beth.

"It's already hot enough to burn you," replied Salome.

Beth had another pang, this time for sun screen. 'They definitely didn't have sun screen in BC,' she thought to herself. She thought again "BC.", this time out loud. Then she shouted, "Luke, I think I know what the clue means!"

"Which clue?"

"You already know what 'doom stone' is about."

"Do I?" said Luke, indolently.

"Anyway, I mean the other clue, the one we thought was a sea with some bees!"

"'Bee sea'? What do you think it means then?"

"Well, I may be wrong, but I think it means 'BC', the time before Christ".

"I remember when Fred announced that from now on BC was to be called BCE in school," recalled Luke.

"Fred?"

"Yes, it was Fred who told us. Don't you remember, my teacher told everyone in the class. His name was Fred".

"Forget Fred," grunted Beth. "We're not interested in our time. What we need to know is something to do with the time before Yeshua was born".

"It's just clicked," said Luke, excitedly. "If BC is the time before Yeshua was born, then there's something about the new age after that which is different. So we need to listen carefully to Simeon and Salome and people as old as them, because they would have been children in BC".

It was all too much to grasp, and as they resumed the journey, Luke went quiet. Maybe it was the sun or the distance they'd walked, but he became rather subdued. Whatever it was, Luke felt the need to think about something other than the clues, so he decided to observe everything he could see around him.

By the time they'd walked into the land beyond the Sea of Salt, they were drained of energy and beginning to experience sore feet. Simeon had thought of going down to the River Jordan to replenish their water supply and bathe their feet but, instead, he decided it would be better to save time and stick to his plan to pick up water supplies from the wadi above Jericho.

Luke looked up at the sky. There weren't any clouds and, as yet, there was no heat haze, but, strangely, the sun felt weaker. Beth traced the look of surprise on her brother's upturned face, so she looked up too, "What are we looking at, Luke?"

Above, in the great arch of the sky, tiny flecks of yellow and white were mixing together in the blue. It didn't look very different, but Luke felt the sun's intensity was draining away. The heat overhead was lessening and a warmth was coming up from the sea and the ground. It had a musty, earthy smell.

"Can you feel the heat coming from the ground, Salome?" he asked.

Salome, always sensitive to a change of mood, hesitated a second. Focusing her eyes after taking a deep breath, she replied, "Yes I can. It smells like the earthy scent of myrrh".

"Yes, I can smell it now," said Simeon. "The earth is giving her heat back the way she does at night".

"But it's day!" shouted Beth.

In the uncertain light, the dry earth and rock seemed as brittle and fragile as a clay pipe about to break. There was an ominous feel to the day, a sense of something in the atmosphere.

Simeon was walking beside Salome, who was rocking gently on the donkey, as Luke and Beth trolled alongside, when something impossible started to happen. Time itself seemed to change round. Darkness was sweeping into the Jordan Valley in the middle of the day. No longer was there a mere sense of foreboding. A change was happening before their eyes.

"What can this be?" demanded Salome, failing to disguise her alarm.

"It's some kind of eclipse of the sun, I think," ventured Luke.

Not knowing what Luke was talking about, Salome turned her frightened eyes on Simeon, wondering whether it was the end of the world. All vestige of light was disappearing and everything around them was plunging into darkness.

Normally the epitome of calm, Salome shouted out, "It's the end of the world!"

"Let's keep moving," shouted Simeon.

As shards of light in the sky faded quickly into mere hints, Salome called back to Simeon, "We need a light!"

"We don't have a lamp, Salome, we have enough to carry as it is," yelled Simeon, whilst mentally mapping out the journey ahead and estimating how long it might take in the dark.

Beth and Luke could hardly believe their eyes, yet there was no mistaking it. Though it seemed impossible, the sun had risen to its highest when the day had suddenly turned into night.

"Now this *is* a sign," said Simeon, conscious that he was now completely lost. Having passed beyond the end of the Sea of Salt, the sound of waves was no longer audible. These sounds would have helped Simeon know how far away from the sea he was. Now he was having trouble working out which way to go.

They stumbled on, not knowing how far they'd travelled, often not knowing whether they were near the track or not. Several times the donkey strayed in a wide curve and, had not Simeon known better, they might easily have ended up going back the way they came.

What had happened just didn't sink in - they simply travelled on, as if it were normal for daylight to disappear at noon. Simeon had intended to turn off along a track that would lead to Jerusalem, but in the darkness, they'd missed it and he felt the best thing to do now was to keep going until they hit Jericho. There was always the danger of losing each other as they wandered on in the dark, so talking to each other definitely seemed a good idea.

Numbed by what had happened, Simeon sought an explanation for it. The daylight sometimes becomes hazy and strange and can even seem to darken a little in the wilderness and there'd been talk in the village about what causes it.

"One of the Jews in our village stood up and told us that God turned the shadow back on the sundial to show King Hezekiah His Word is true," said Simeon.

"You mean God changed time," said Beth.

"No, that can't happen!" said Luke.

"Tell me what else is happening, if it's not the end of the world?" asked Salome, almost hysterical.

"It's an eclipse of the sun. Every now and then the moon gets in the way of the sun as it moves across the sky," explained Luke, "and the sunlight is blocked out".

"So it goes dark?" said Beth.

"Yes".

"And how long does that last?" asked Salome, longing for the light to return.

"An eclipse of the sun lasts about five minutes," replied Luke, repeating almost word for word what he'd learned from a science film. "And it's never as long as ten minutes".

Simeon put together what had been said, "Well, there's been no light here for nearly half an hour now, so it can't be an eclipse".

"What a precious thing is light?" moaned Salome. "Without it, you totter in the darkness, you lose your way.".

Simeon stopped her, "We don't want to hear that now, Salome. What we need now is hope".

"Yes, we hope we'll come out of this," said Beth.

"You have hope then, Beth?" asked Salome, brightly, thinking Beth had found something.

"What I mean is that I hope things will improve," answered Beth.

"No," said Salome, "hope is when you believe something that is certain to happen".

A few seconds later, Luke, who was walking faster than anyone else, tripped on a rock and fell headlong.

"Well. I think _that_ was always going to happen," giggled Beth. They all stopped and hauled Luke to his feet.

Luke had been listening so intently that he hadn't been watching where he was going. Rubbing the dirt from his knees, he looked up and said, "You can't hope for something certain because if it's in the future you don't know whether it's going to happen or not".

Everyone went quiet and Luke felt sure everyone had realized that he was right, until Simeon said something from the other side of the donkey and they all had to try hard to listen.

"I want to tell you about the Hope of Israel. It's a real definite hope that the Jews believe will come true," he said.

"And do you believe that hope?" asked Beth.

"It's not for me, it's their hope that the Messiah will definitely come, but they don't know when".

"Well something has definitely come today!" cried Salome.

Simeon changed tack, "Listen, here's something else. A silk trader from the East told me that a traveller coming in the opposite direction greeted him and said he had some very valuable goods in his possession. The silk trader grew curious and asked what they were and the traveller said he would take a sample out and leave it on the ground in front of him, but only if the silk trader closed his eyes and tried to guess what the goods were".

"What happened?" asked Luke, now interested.

"The silk trader closed his eyes and eventually said, 'it's a goblet of gold'. The traveller said, 'No, it isn't. Give me a minute to put another sample out instead just in case you've seen the first one …Now, try again'. The silk trader said, 'It's a necklace of pearls'. This time there was no answer. After a while, he opened his eyes to find that there was no-one there".

"What did he do then?" asked Beth.

"He looked around".

"And what did he see?" she asked.

"That his goods had all been stolen".

Simeon failed to notice that as he told the story, Luke had not only guessed the ending, but also cheekily led the donkey quietly away into the darkness. Simeon turned round to reach for the lead only to find it was gone. As he stood there, wondering what had happened, Luke reappeared with the donkey and said, "I had you worried".

"Come on you two, there's nothing funny about the situation we're in", said Salome. "We need to find a way out of the darkness".

"How do you find the way to the light?" asked Beth.

"You find the tiniest speck of light and you travel nearer and nearer to it until it becomes bigger," said Salome with that allure in her voice they'd grown used to, a softness and a warmth that made them want to listen.

"The light is the light," she said, "the darkness is the darkness. They say Israel's God is more brilliant than the sun, so bright you cannot even look. Do you think we should ask the Jews for guidance?"

"If we meet one," replied Luke with a deadpan voice.

"What do you believe, Salome?" asked Beth.

"I believe the light is the light, it is definite," she spoke straight from her heart, treating Beth's question with respect. "I believe the Jews have a definite hope, something they are certain is true, not something they wish but are not sure will come true. As for me, I'd like some definite hope that we're going to see daylight again".

Luke pressed her further, "So what do you really believe right now?"

"I feel like it's the end of the world," she said, being honest.

"I think I can help you there, Salome," said Beth. "It can't be the end of the world because we're from the future and, believe it or not, the world is still here in two thousand years' time!"

"There you are, Salome," said Simeon. "That's definite hope".

Salome smiled and breathed a sigh of relief.

Centurion Justinus Jacumas had received orders at Herod's Palace in Jericho, to take a detachment of soldiers up to Jerusalem to find out what the man they called the Governor had to say about the present darkness.

In the well-lit Reception Hall of Herod's Jericho Palace, most staff moved briskly in the knowledge that there was an emergency, even though there didn't seem to be anything anybody could do about it.

Justinus Jacumas, who was new to Jericho, asked a stressed-looking Roman official at the palace, whether there was anything among the meticulously compiled documents of instructions sent from Rome, to tell them what to do when the world is plunged into complete darkness in the middle of the day. He was told in no uncertain terms that no instructions were currently available.

The advice that he did receive at the palace was to be careful not to take his men up the Wadi Qelt, the canyon which opens out on to Herod's Palace and Jericho. He was also advised not to take any torches so that the men might move around more easily, without causing undue alarm by appearing out of the darkness and provoking panic among the people. There was enough chaos in Jericho as it was.

Emerging from Herod's Palace, he looked up at the sky, searching for reasons why the darkness had come. But, as a Roman soldier under orders he had to put aside his questions and focus on what he had been given to do. He told himself that whatever the gods had done to make the day night, he simply needed to complete his task and get a detachment of men up to Jerusalem, in double quick time.

His second-in-command, an *optio*, was waiting outside the palace with forty soldiers. "Do you want me to take them to Jerusalem?" he asked.

"No," replied Justinus. "I'm seeking an audience with the Governor there. He won't listen to an *optio* like you. Keep the rest of the men occupied. You can patrol the town and try to bring calm to the streets, but don't be heavy-handed. We don't want a rebellion here".

Justinus turned and urged all forty men onward into the darkness beyond Herod's Palace. From the start, it was almost impossible to keep to the road, which had only opened a few years before when Herod's Palace was built. It wasn't his only palace but it was new. There hadn't been time for the roadway to Jerusalem to be worn into a clear track yet.

Before long, it became obvious that they were lost. The land fell away into the canyon of Wadi Qelt to their right and they'd been so careful in avoiding it, they'd wandered further off to the left than they should have done. Justinus caught a glimpse of the lights of Jericho and Herod's Palace far below, but had no choice but to lead them onward.

Ten minutes later, Justinus and his soldiers were still trying to circle round to the right, in order to find the edge of the canyon.

Nearby, they heard the sound of voices. Justinus drew his men together and ordered them to move as silently as possible.

"If you come up against them do not break cover," was his next command. "You are to shadow them quietly as they move along, until you receive either an order to strike or an order to make contact.

· · · · · · · · ● · · · · · · · · · ·

Trying to find the way ahead in darkness, was soaking up all Simeon's energy. As he trudged carefully along, he was straining his eyes for a glimpse of the wadi.

When Simeon stopped again, Luke called to him, "Do you know which way to go?"

"Yes, I know which way to go," said Simeon gruffly.

Despite being in a situation that Simeon would not have expected in his wildest dreams, Beth and Luke had to admit that Simeon was their best hope. There was something about him that gave Beth and Luke the belief that they would be safe. He thought so thoroughly about how to do things, although not so much about everyone else. If anyone could find the way and make things all right, it would be him. However, Salome, the person who knew him best, was not so sure.

"I feel completely powerless because what is happening is happening to the cosmos and there's nothing we can do about it," she declared.

Nevertheless, Salome's tone was calmer than before. She was spared from complete despair in the sure knowledge that the world would last another two thousand years.

"We need to find Wadi Qelt," grinned Simeon, trying to bring things down to earth.

It was clear no-one else had a plan. What Simeon knew was that as long as they kept walking forward, they would reach a stream flowing from the springs in Wadi Qelt, or bump into the aqueduct which carried water from Wadi Qelt to the city of Jericho.

Behind them, Luke and Beth were talking, trying to fathom time, when out of nowhere, a sound like the clattering of swords against shields brought everyone to a standstill.

7

IN THE MIDST OF THIEVES

Listening in the darkness, with their hearts in their mouths, Luke, Beth, Salome and Simeon heard no trace of the sound again. All had gone quiet as, creeping at first, they began to move again.

"The donkey won't be able to go much farther without a rest," announced Simeon.

The donkey had been blundering along, off-road through a rocky wilderness, for more than an hour. Salome had been walking beside her, coaxing every ounce of effort from the poor animal.

"She's exhausted. This is cruel," complained Salome, as she poked her husband in the back, "Simeon, we definitely need to call a halt now. The donkey is completely exhausted".

Simeon appeared not to hear. "Simeon, the donkey's about to collapse, we need to stop!"

Simeon relented. "I have just said so, Salome, but we do need to be nearer to Wadi Qelt first, because we're going to get some water from the stream down there, for us and the donkey".

What Simeon did not tell them was that the stream was guarded by huge cliffs and there were only certain places where you could get down to it. Also, he failed to mention that he had no idea whether there was a safe way down from where he was standing.

Arriving at a place where the ground fell away, Simeon discovered they'd reached the gorge of Wadi Qelt.

"Let's all stay by the donkey and have a rest here," suggested Salome, "and let Simeon go down to the Wadi by himself".

"That would be best," said Simeon. "Getting down there may be dangerous".

Simeon reached into the pack on the donkey and found the wineskin, then turned into the darkness. As soon as he was gone, Salome started to worry, and she called out after him, "Watch your step!"

"I'll be all right!"

Simeon may have thought he would be all right, but, if he'd stopped to think about it, he'd have to admit that he had little chance of reaching the stream.

In spite of this, Simeon put danger out of mind and steadily made his way downhill. Before long, he saw ahead a block of even blacker darkness. He stopped and tried to work out what it was. It could be either a sheer drop down to the bottom of the wadi, a big rock rising in front of him, or a massive cave. As he moved towards it, his shoulder hit an overhang of rock and he reeled backwards in pain. Running his hand along the rough edge of the overhang, he found that it continued higher up, in the shape of an arch or perhaps a cave entrance.

Simeon suddenly recalled talking to Luke and Beth about the Stone of Doom. Gripped by the thought that if he walked farther, he might step into a cave, he stood there, frozen, not knowing whether to inch forward or not.

Remembering the sound they'd heard earlier, like swords being beaten on shields, his mind began to play tricks on him. Maybe it was just now that he'd heard the sound. Perhaps there were hidden soldiers, lurking in the dark, ready to roll a stone behind him the moment he took another step.

Simeon stayed still, trying to soften the sound of his own breath. Slowly, he looked around and listened as hard as possible. Then he allowed himself a count of one to five before making his mind up about whether he would take a stride into nothingness.

One…two…three…four…five, Simeon stepped but tripped over an edge.

Simeon was bumping and sliding downwards, desperately trying to grab hold of something, tearing his hands on whatever rocks were in his clutch, yet they slipped from his grasp. He skidded helplessly downward, until he was jolted and flung on to his side, rolling over again and again until he came to a stop.

All was silent as he lay there in shock.

Looking around, he waited for his eyes to acclimatise to the darkness. It was then he felt a numbness in his knee and a dull pain in his left leg.

To his right, an inky black shape soared up above him. After a while, he felt his legs for bruises. They were sore but he could not feel the warmth and wetness of blood. Looking up again, he began to realize that the large, looming shape above him, just to the right, was actually a cliff. Fortunately for him, he had narrowly missed falling over the top of it. Instead, he'd slipped down the steep slope beside it.

Soon Simeon realised he could move and he started to crawl further down, heading for the bottom of the wadi.

When he felt bushes brushing up against him, he managed to pick himself up and, limping, rustled through them until he heard the soft, rushing sound of a stream.

Running, half stumbling, he splashed over a shimmering thread of water making its way down the wadi. Following the stream, he came upon a pool deep enough to fill the skin with water.

Simeon tied up the water-filled skin and laid it down by the side of the stream. Then he reached into the water. Cupping his palms together, he scooped the water into his mouth and drank and drank until his thirst was quenched.

Refreshed, he sat back, sweat pouring down his face. Now he began to wonder how he was going to get out of the place.

Rather than search for an easier way, he decided to retrace his steps back up the slope he'd fallen down, to make sure he had the chance of returning to exactly where he started, where the others would be. Although it was a very steep way up, at least he would know what was there. Simeon slung the wineskin over his shoulder and tied it to the sash around his waist. Then he moved off in the direction of the slope he'd fallen down.

Scrambling upwards, the slope felt even steeper than when he'd come careering down it. Stones and dust turned into rocks, as he climbed, but the rocks soon became steeper and Simeon found himself searching for footholds in the dark, then handholds to pull himself up, until it became too difficult to climb at all, with a wineskin of water dangling over his shoulder.

With one last lunge he reached up for another hold, but the rock came away in his hand. Losing his balance, Simeon rocked backwards on his feet and held on with one hand. It took him every last ounce of energy to pull forward again and keep contact with the cliff. His heart was thumping in his chest, as the wineskin swayed back and forth. This was surely the cliff he'd seen on the way down, he thought, but now he was imprisoned on it.

Simeon leant further into the cliff, trying to think, with muscles aching as he held the strain. What could he do? He was trapped here and soon the three at the top of the wadi would be worrying that he might not be coming back.

After what seemed a lifetime in the situation, he closed his eyes and told himself that what he'd done was stray away from the slope on the left that he'd been climbing. There was nothing else for it, but to find a way across the broken rocks to his left, toward that slope and then carry on going upwards until he reached the top of the wadi.

· · · · · · ●●● ● ●●● · · · · · ·

"Simeon's been gone too long," Salome whispered to Beth and Luke, as they huddled round the donkey. "Let's call his name out and see if he's there".

"Simeon, are you there?" called Luke. Everyone stood up to listen for a reply, but his shout was met by silence.

"Have you found the stream yet?" Beth's words disappeared into the air.

"Simeon, Simeon," bawled Salome.

They shouted and shouted, but there was no answer. Salome suggested they go down and find him. She was beside herself.

"Wouldn't we get lost too," said Luke sensibly.

"What else can we do?" screeched Beth.

"Right," said Salome, chastened into action. "I can stay with the donkey while you both look for Simeon. Then there'll be someone to help if one of you gets into trouble".

Beth and Luke were petrified but they agreed to do it. They held hands together and slowly moved downward towards the confines of the wadi. If they hadn't already had the experience of finding their way down those slopes in the wilderness, they probably would have given up, but somehow they found the grit to go ahead and step down into a rocky darkness, not knowing what they would find. Moving as carefully as possible, they began shouting Simeon's name, but screaming at silence was eerie.

The slope steepened and now each shout had an echo. "Let's shout back to Salome so she knows we're all right," said Beth.

"Salome, we're OK".

Shout as they may, nothing could be heard from the top. Luke and Beth realised they were now isolated and probably lost. Nevertheless, they pressed on downward until they saw a large jet-black shape below them. Making their way toward it, it soon appeared to be right in front of them.

"Shall I step into it?" asked Luke.

"No. Luke, put your hand out and see what it is".

Luke shuffled forwards on his knees and put his hand out to touch it, but there was nothing there. He called back to Beth, "It's just thin air".

"Let's not go any further," warned Beth, "in case we have an accident".

"I think there's a big drop here," said Luke, gazing below him.

Luke and Beth had just turned round to go back when they heard a weak voice that could easily have been the sound of a bird. Again it cried, followed by a flutter of wings.

"Beth, that could have been Simeon making a sound and disturbing an animal".

Beth wasn't convinced, "It sounded like a bird squawking and flying, if you ask me".

"Simeon, we're over here!" they cried, hoping it was him. There was no answer.

They waited, five minutes, ten minutes, shouting out his name every so often, but still there was no reply. Reluctantly, they decided to head back. It would be no mean feat just to get back to the top of the wadi and find where Salome and the donkey were. They tried calling out again.

"Salome, can you hear us?"

"Salome are you there?"

"Yes!" It was Salome.

"We shouted out for Simeon," said Beth, as they joined her at the top of the slope.

"Don't give up," pleaded Salome.

"We're over here, Simeon!"

"Here!!"

"Simeon!! Simeon!!"

Luke took in a big lungful of air and bellowed, "We are here!!!"

A moment later, a quiet voice spoke, "Yes, I know".

Everyone looked round to see where it came from and there, standing by a frightened donkey, was Simeon, covered in sweat and dust, holding a skin of water for them to drink.

"Save some," he said as they slaked their thirsts. "It's still a long way to Jerusalem".

"That water tastes so good," beamed Luke. "We heard a bird call and fly overhead. Did you hear it, Simeon?"

"No".

"I told you," said Beth to Luke. "Birds probably can't live down there, anyway".

"They can," said Simeon. "There is every chance you might have heard a bird. Did you know the prophet Elijah found ravens or rather they found him, in a wadi like this that flows into the Jordan?"

"I didn't even know that there was a prophet Elijah," replied Luke.

"What do they teach you in two thousand years' time?" despaired Simeon.

"Would you like some raisin cakes?" asked Salome.

"This is no place to stay," warned Simeon. "The sooner we move the better".

As they set out again, walking was easier. Having been hemmed in by dark cliffs, Luke, Beth and Simeon's eyes were now more accustomed to the lack of light out in the open.

Suddenly, Luke thought he'd heard something.

"Did you hear that noise…look over there?"

"Luke, we can't see in the darkness".

"Just keep going," said Simeon, as they trod along behind each other.

"It sounded like a rock hitting a rock. I'm not making it up," insisted Luke.

Suddenly, there was a clattering of equipment on rock and, there in front of them, like an army coming out of the mist, about ten Roman legionaries appeared amidst the rocks. A well-armed soldier rapped the ground with a twisted stick, and stood there in fearsome array. "That one's the centurion", whispered Simeon to Luke.

"In the name of Emperor Tiberius Caesar Augustus," he announced, "where are you going?"

"To Jerusalem", stuttered Simeon. There was one long moment when it seemed they were about to be attacked or arrested but, instead, the centurion took off his helmet and rested it in the bend of his arm, declaring, "I am Centurion Justinus Jacumus, under orders to march to Jerusalem. Are you going in that direction?"

"We are," replied Simeon.

The centurion waved his vine stick and everyone sat on the ground. The centurion then invited Simeon to sit down next to him. Centurion Justinus Jacumas had been in some spots during his time in Israel, but he'd never been as close-up and personal with the inhabitants as this. He decided to make a virtue of necessity and treat Simeon well, in case he could be of any help.

"Who are you?"

"My name is Simeon, I'm a trader from near the Sea of Salt," confided Simeon.

"We have been moving very slowly," said the Centurion. "When we set out from Herod's palace in Jericho the whole world darkened and that's what held us up".

He seemed dazed and reluctant to say any more, so Simeon asked him a question: "Is Jericho your base?"

"No, we came down from Tiberias".

"The new city by the Sea of Galilee?"

"Yes, that's the one".

"But you've come from Jericho?"

"Yes, we stopped outside Jericho last night and now it's night again," he said, trying to come to terms with what had happened, "and we've been wandering all over the place until we came across you".

"And what did you think of the city of Jericho?" asked Simeon.

Justinus was a man who spent his time giving orders or receiving orders, so it was refreshing to be asked what he thought about something. He told Simeon about the people who had come out on to the streets of Jericho, when the darkness came. As he opened up, he warmed to Simeon's company.

"Simeon, you can join us, if you wish".

"Will it be safe to do so?" asked Simeon.

"You and your family will be safe with us. You have my word on it," said Justinus, looking slightly surprised at the odd wash-faded clothes Beth and Luke were wearing. Simeon toyed with the idea of explaining, but he knew it was beyond him.

Justinus signalled to his men that it was time to move.

Luke had only recently read a book about meeting Romans from the past and now he could only shake his head with disbelief to think he was with Roman soldiers, who were about to march in thick darkness, at lunch time.

As they walked over the rocks, the scraping and crashing of the hobnails in the legionaries' boots gave some indication of how many there were. Luke nudged Beth, "I think there are about fifty soldiers".

After twenty minutes or so, they slowed down.

"Simeon can you let me have a drink from the wineskin?" rasped Salome.

"Let's all have some," suggested Simeon.

The Centurion had already stopped in his tracks, hesitant about which way to go. Seeing that Simeon had slowed down, he came and sat with him, ordering a halt.

"How are things in Galilee?" asked Simeon.

"Thousands of people have been gathering in different places this last year or two. They meet anywhere, on a hillside, by the lake or near their homes and synagogues. They listen to a man who heals them".

"Who is he?"

"His name is Yeshua".

"Oh, yes, we've heard about him down here too".

"In Capernaum, near us, a centurion's daughter was paralysed and troubled in spirit and he was asked to heal her".

"What happened?"

"So this centurion in Caesar's Imperial Army said he wasn't worthy enough for Yeshua to come to his house. Instead, he said that just as he, a centurion, gave orders which were obeyed elsewhere, so Yeshua, whose authority he recognised, need only speak the word and his daughter would be healed even though she was in another place".

"And, did he?"

"Yeshua told the centurion it would happen just the way the centurion believed it would and she was healed that very moment!"

"What is this?" said Simeon. "At the very moment a centurion realises he is unworthy and acknowledges it, then Yeshua answers his deepest longing and heals his daughter".

Justinus himself had a question that he had been too proud to ask until now. Having talked about the centurion who was humble enough to say he wasn't worthy to have a Galilean ex-carpenter as a guest in his home, surely he, Justinus, could ask for the help of an ordinary trader to guide his troop into Jerusalem.

"Have you been this way to Jerusalem before?"

"Yes, many times," Simeon replied.

"Can you guide me to Jerusalem?" asked the Centurion, as a lump rose in his throat.

"I would be glad to take you to Jerusalem, it's a well-trodden road", said Simeon, neglecting to mention that he wasn't so confident he could do it in the dark.

As if Simeon didn't have enough problems, now he was putting himself under pressure to lead a troop of soldiers in the dark, with a Roman centurion breathing down his neck.

· · · · · · · · · · ● · · · · · · · · · · ·

It wasn't a normal day for a thief. Inexplicable and awesome though the daytime darkness was, it was also an opportunity. Josiah and his band of robbers couldn't believe their luck.

Many people who wouldn't be around at night time, were travelling to Jerusalem in the day time. Because of the spectacular disappearance of the sun, it was going to be easy to ambush them.

The gang set themselves up on both sides of the road, a short distance below Bethany, and waited.

"It won't be long now before people pass by," shouted Josiah to his men. "We only go for them if they're walking. If not, keep quiet until they've gone. The signal is when I step out in front of them to ask how far it is to Jericho or Jerusalem".

This is going to be easy said the robbers among themselves as they settled behind rocks and in hollows. No-one felt any nerves, that was, until the earth moved under their feet.

"Did you feel that?" said Josiah to the other robbers, hidden round about him. 'Perhaps we shouldn't do this,' he whispered to himself. Then he pushed the thought out of his mind.

A strange thing happened, as he called them to his side. The sky grew pale above and the darkness changed to grey shadows. Before long, they began to make out the shapes of four people coming up the road from Jericho. One was riding a donkey.

One of the thieves leaned over to Josiah. "Someone is riding, shall we let these go by?"

"What are you asking?" sighed Josiah, looking at the load as it wobbled on the donkey's back with Beth drooped over the top of it. "Do you think we should run away from a tired child on a donkey?"

"No, but…". Josiah cut him short and now that the light had increased enough for him to see them all, he signalled to the others to be attentive.

He stepped out in front of the four people and declared, rather improbably, "You're going to show me the way to Jerusalem".

Just then Josiah's men rushed out with swords and clubs and stood by each person. Dramatically, two of them seized the donkey. The donkey put up no opposition at all and didn't bray once about being brought to a standstill.

"Give us the donkey and its load or you'll all be killed," screamed Josiah, with the first beams of daylight falling upon his face revealing what he looked like.

"No, it is you who will be killed!" shouted Justinus, as forty Roman legionaries stood up and showed their blades.

"The *gladius* blades, glinting in the daylight, were enough to put Josiah and his thieves to flight. Pursued by the soldiers, they scattered, each man for himself, dropping their clubs and swords as they went, so as to run faster.

"Stop the chase!" bellowed Justinus. "Stay compact, We must fast march to Jerusalem now". To a man they turned round, and came back as a column. The day had returned to them and the road ahead was clear.

The men fell into a tight formation a short distance up the road. Justinus turned to Simeon, struck the left side of his breast soundly with the palm of his hand and affirmed, "May the gods be with you".

"Oh, they will be, but not with those rascals," roared Simeon.

"I saw their leader's face. I will recognise and deal with him when I see him again," promised Justinus, "but now I must march on to Jerusalem on an urgent errand".

And, with that, he swivelled round and walked away, stepping up his pace until he reached the body of men.

Taking up his place at the head of the column, he ordered them forward along the road to Bethany and Jerusalem.

As Beth watched them go, she asked, "What made the ground shake?"

"It all happened so quickly," gasped Salome, feeling uncertain again. "Something is happening to the cosmos",

"It's not the end of the world, though, is it?" Luke reminded her.

"It was incredible to see the light come just in time for us to see the look on the thieves' faces, when the Romans appeared," said Beth.

"Especially when their leader's face dropped," chuckled Simeon.

"One second he was the bandits' hero, the next he was a zero!" laughed Luke.

Laugh as he may, the thieves were still on Simeon's mind. They could come back, now the Romans had left, at any moment. Considering the danger they may be in, he sensed the need to move off as soon as possible.

"Let's go," he said, "we won't get to Jerusalem until we start to move. Come on, put one foot in front of the other!".

For much of the journey to Bethany and beyond, Beth and Luke teased one another, blocking each other's path and saying, "I put one foot in front of the other foot," only to walk off quickly, nose in the air, as if superior to the other person.

Somewhere between Bethany and Jerusalem, children passed by, coming from the other direction with their parents, on their way to Bethany. Salome noticed that each child appeared to have been upset by something, so she stopped one of the mothers, to ask why.

"They took Yeshua, They took him away," she said. The hurt in her eyes and the look on the children's faces, led Salome to suspect the worst. The family moved off, but more people were coming, so Salome and Simeon looked for someone who might tell them more about what had happened.

A man stopped for a moment, waiting for his children to catch up, he'd been walking quickly and was almost breathless.

"Where did they take Yeshua?" asked Simeon.

The man could hardly speak. "They took him to Golgotha, the place of the skull, to be crucified along with two thieves. One of them mocked him, but the other acknowledged that Yeshua was innocent of any crime".

"How can this be, that he should suffer when he harmed no-one?" groaned Salome.

The children came up and gathered close to their father. Their mother arrived, panting. After resting a minute or two, she was still breathing heavily. Salome noticed that there was another baby on the way.

"He wept when his friend Lazarus died," she said. "Then he raised Lazarus to life. Martha told him he could do it because he is the Christ".

Just as soon as they had come, the people walking toward them had all gone, leaving Simeon and Salome to wonder what it was all about.

Turning round, they set their sights on Jerusalem.

"Time for you to have a ride again, Beth," called Salome, invitingly.

Luke came and helped Beth on to the donkey. It wasn't long before it was the donkey's turn for a rest, or so thought Beth. She asked to be helped down and the four of them continued walking toward Jerusalem, leading the tired donkey behind them.

As the day wore on, Beth and Luke found they had nothing to say about what had upset the people who'd passed by on their way to Bethany. It wasn't as if they didn't care, it's just that there was nothing they could say.

"So Yeshua is the Christ," said Beth, trying to work things out.

"Yes, he *is* Jesus Christ," answered Luke.

In the twenty first century, Beth and Luke had heard one or two stories about Jesus Christ, but just now on the road, it felt as if he'd come near. No-one had spoken about him with such raw feeling as those heartbroken families on the road to Bethany.

What were they to make of all this?

SYMBOL OF COURAGE

His headaches were over – being stranded on a cliff without any light, leading a crowd of people through the dark under the close attention of a Roman centurion, the earth shaking, and facing up to a bunch of thieves at first light – it was all over. With almost every step, Beth and Luke could see Simeon's face brightening. Now all he had to do was put one foot in front of the other, and soon they would be in Jerusalem.

Simeon had no way of understanding the strange nocturnal occurrence that had taken place that day, but what he did know was that he couldn't wait to show the city to his new friends.

Salome had noticed the change too. She could see there was a spring in his step. Simeon had quickened his pace. Beth and Luke were no longer running ahead, doing silly walks. They were alongside the donkey now, with Simeon marching relentlessly forward.

As he speeded up, the donkey slowed down. Her load was wobbling about more and more. Salome, walking beside her, reached to see if the tie around the donkey's belly had loosened. No-one had checked it since the thieves had their hands on it. It looked all right, but as soon as she touched it, the tie came undone and cloths and spices tumbled to the ground.

Simeon turned to see what had happened, slapped his forehead as if to say 'What next?', and cried out, "Stop!"

Beth and Luke scurried back dutifully to help gather up his wares, whilst Simeon repacked everything. Salome was standing around waiting, still thinking about how helpful the Romans were in rescuing them from the thieves. She wondered why they would do that, perhaps it was because they wanted to save Simeon so he could guide them, or perhaps it was just an accident that they'd suddenly appeared as the light came. The Romans would be with you, she reflected, as long as it helped their Empire.

On the way to Jerusalem, Salome had time to think about it. Simeon and Justinus appeared to have struck up a good friendship, but was that simply out of necessity? For the Roman detachment, Simeon was the ticket out of a mess they'd got themselves into, so perhaps it was just a friendship of convenience. As soon as light returned, the detachment had moved off at top speed to Jerusalem.

Salome wondered if there had been any real friendship between Justinus and Simeon at all.

When the gate of Jerusalem came into sight, Simeon smiled broadly. "There's the Temple Mount." he said, pointing toward it. "I'll take you there".

Salome interrupted more mundanely, "Through the South Gate and just to the left, is where Sara lives, and that's where we'll be staying".

"Jerusalem does look a big place," said Beth, her dogged grin softening into a surprised smile. However, the thought of having a rest in someone's house was much more appealing to her, than going on a tour of the city.

"Some sad things have happened here today," said Luke, remembering the news they'd heard on the way from Bethany, which they hadn't been able to talk about. If this had been a hint for Simeon to explain what that was all about, it fell on deaf ears. Simeon was intent on passing through the South Gate and showing them every sight he could, though perhaps he would save the Temple Mount for tomorrow.

Shortly after they'd entered the city, they stopped near the Pool of Siloam to agree together what to do next. Simeon was clear about what he wanted to do. "I say we go up the Tyropoean valley".

Salome prickled. "No!" she said. "We need to go to Sara's and rest the donkey". Looking closely at Simeon, hoping to catch his attention, she studied his face for some understanding of how everyone else was feeling. "We're all tired and hungry, so it's best to go to Sara's and she'll give us something to eat".

"Can't we go the long way – up the Tyropoean valley, across to the bazaar and back down to Sara's that way? It's not far to go".

"No!" said Salome, putting her foot down. "We're tired. I haven't come here to look around, but to be with family," she protested.

"What do you think Luke and Beth?" asked Simeon. "What would you like to do?"

"Go to Sara's and rest," sighed Beth.

"Yes," agreed Luke, "Something to eat would be good".

Crestfallen, Simeon accepted defeat. The city would have to wait. Walking at low speed, leading a very tired donkey, they made their way into the poorest district of Jerusalem to meet up with cousin Sara.

Sara's house was unremarkable, but what was lacking she made up for in kindness. She greeted everyone warmly and instantly made them feel at home. Sara told them she was waiting for her husband Idris to bring something to eat. Idris hadn't come home yet from selling spices in the market place.

Idris had started the day at his usual pitch by the Temple Mount but most people who'd been up on the Temple Mount had gone down to join the crowds surging through the streets to find out what was going to happen to Yeshua after he'd been tried by the chief priests and elders who supposed him guilty, despite the fact that the trial witness accounts didn't stack up with each other.

The chief priests and elders passed his case on to Pontius Pilate the Roman Governor, hoping his authority would make it stick. But when Pilate went soft on them and told the crowd he couldn't see anything wrong with Yeshua, their hopes took a dip.

There was a custom for one person to be set free at the Passover, and Pilate asked the crowd if they would like him to release Yeshua. Those intent on seeing sentence passed on him were pressed up close to proceedings, yelling as loud as they could. Pilate listened to those who shouted the loudest.

It looked like the people could have gone either way, but the chief priests and elders urged the crowd to shout for Barabbas to be the one set free. Barabbas had led a rebellion against Roman rule in Jerusalem and the many people in the crowd who felt resentment about being ruled by the Romans, were now given a way of expressing it without getting into any trouble.

So it was that Pontius Pilate, a Roman, ended up setting free a man who wanted to kill Romans. As Yeshua stood by the Governor, it was clear that a mock trial had descended into chaos. Even if Pontius Pilate the Governor had wanted to save Yeshua, he had already gone too far in allowing the crowd to become both judge and jury. The Romans took him to Golgotha and carried out the death sentence.

A few hours later, a trickle of trade had returned to the market and some traders were selling a few of their wares, but no-one bought any spices from Idris. Yet he refused to go home, not even an earthquake (and there was one) would make him leave until he'd sold enough to buy food to put on the table at home.

· · · · · · · · · · ● · · · · · · · · · · ·

Centurion Justinus Jacumas and his band of men had reached Herod's Palace in Jerusalem on foot from Herod's Palace in Jericho. He was not proud about the way the journey had turned out and, alongside the soldiers by the Jerusalem Palace, rather than talk about his meandering march from Jericho, Justinus chose to listen to another centurion who was talking to an *optio* about what they had been doing during the three hours of darkness.

"Do either of you know what happened to Yeshua of Nazareth?" asked Justinus.

"He'd been given a hearing with the chief priests, then they sent him to Herod's Palace", said the *optio*, "to give more weight to their case as Yeshua is from Galilee and Herod has jurisdiction there".

"I know, I'm stationed in Galilee," said Justinus.

"Did you ever meet Yeshua there?" asked the *optio*.

"I heard the laughter and saw the tears as they listened to every word he spoke, but no, not personally. What happened to Yeshua at the Palace?"

"Having heard so much about him, King Herod wanted Yeshua to show him a miracle and tell him many things".

"What did Yeshua do?"

"He stayed silent".

"That doesn't sound a wise thing to do when a king asks a question, but I suppose a king could show mercy".

"Yes, but when do they?"

"When they feel like it, I suppose," said Justinus. "How well did Herod treat him?"

The *optio* shook his head, "It's unbelievable that you can treat a good man like that".

"Like what?"

"Well, I think," said the *optio*, "that when Yeshua wouldn't answer his questions, Herod and his men started to mock him and they dressed him in a gorgeous robe and laughed at him".

"And did that upset you?" asked Justinus, detecting a slight waver in the *optio*'s voice.

"Yes, it did. The chief priests and scribes were there, arguing a case against him, accusing him, trying to influence Herod's opinion."

"What was your opinion about it?" asked Justinus.

The *optio* frowned, "I didn't know what to think. I just stood there listening to their fierce allegations".

Justinus turned to the centurion, "And where were you, centurion?"

"I was there at the cross".

"We were on the road to Jerusalem when the darkness came," said Justinus.

What had seemed to Justinus like an epic, now seemed little more than small talk, as the centurion started to speak.

"If you had stood where I stood by the cross and had heard him say, 'Father forgive them for they know not what they do,' after darkness had swept the land and the earth had shaken violently, then you would have understood that truly he is the Son of God".

Justinus was moved by what the centurion had said, but the *optio* was incensed by it all. He looked despitefully in the direction of Herod's throne, "They are called rulers, but they could not rule him. Part of them wanted to be nice to Yeshua but they weren't able to do it, because they couldn't even rule themselves".

"What are you talking about? Kings can give orders," said Justinus.

"Kings in palaces may think they rule the world by giving orders, while doing nothing themselves, but it's us on the ground that have to do their dirty work".

"You're a child of Rome and you're expected to do your duty if you want to be a Roman citizen," said Justinus. "What have you to say in your defence?"

"That they crucified an innocent man," said the *optio*.

Justinus held his peace. After a while he spoke, "Well," he paused, "his fate is sealed now".

"And who knows if we'll see his like again?" breathed the *optio*.

It had been the strangest of days. Sara pulled down the lamp from the hook and checked to see if there was enough oil in it.

Beth and Luke were learning how to sing a song that Salome knew, but it was nothing like anything they had ever heard.

As she lit the lamp, Sara was secretly worrying that daylight might not come back in the morning.

When the singing stopped, Sara sat down quietly to listen to what Salome and Simeon had to say about their journey to Jerusalem.

"So, where were you when it went dark?" she asked.

"We'd left the Sea of Salt and we were not far from Jericho. Believe it or not, Simeon kept us mostly on track." Salome gave Simeon an acknowledging look of gratitude, "but, as for me, I thought it was the end of the world".

"So did I!" said Sara. "It happened at the same time that Yeshua died. His followers said he was the Messiah, the Christ, and then this happened".

"Remind me what we need to know about 'Before Christ'?" whispered Luke to Beth.

Beth thought for a while, as Salome, Simeon and Sara continued talking on the other side of the room. Then she sidled up to Luke and said, "It's because there's a big difference between BC and AD and Christ has something to do with it".

"It must be the difference between the ancient world and the modern world we live in," replied Luke.

"If you say so," said Beth, "but that makes me none the wiser".

Thinking about what he had meant, Luke pictured Gandalf the wizard with his staff, striking a huge monster of the ancient world in order to prevent it blocking a narrow bridge over a vast chasm. The monster fell from the bridge and, for a moment it seemed the wizard had won, but with one great upward sway of its long tail the monster hooked its tail tip around Gandalf and threw him off the bridge and down into the abyss below. Before he had time to put this into words for Beth, a tall figure crept into the house.

It was Idris. He looked over toward Simeon, "Your donkey is in a sorry state," he said. "I took her to the field we use. She needs to stay there a week or two before she gets her strength up".

"Thank you, Idris, that was thoughtful of you".

Idris squashed his baggage against the wall, and everyone shuffled up for him in the confined space.

"What was all that, that happened today?" he asked, still trying to make sense of it.

"We don't know," said Sara, "We were talking about it just now".

"We didn't think we were going to make it here until we actually walked through the South Gate, and ended up at the pool that Simeon called Siloam," continued Salome, "and what with darkness in the middle of the day and thinking I'd lost my husband and him leading part of the Roman Army on their way to Jerusalem and being attacked by thieves, Simeon then goes and says he'd like to spend an hour or two taking us all round Jerusalem!"

"Not to mention the earthquake," added Sara.

"We had a bit of a row," admitted Simeon. "Salome was right, we should have come to your house first. But now, what's this I hear about Yeshua dying?"

"That's what I was going to tell you when I came in," answered Idris.

"But you were polite and listened to us first," said Salome, who made a habit of noticing little things.

"Yes, well, you learn to listen to people in the market place".

"Is that where you've been today?" asked Salome.

"Yes," replied Idris, "but with what was happening in Jerusalem and those hours of darkness, it was hard to sell".

"Did you sell anything at all?" Between his words, Sara was reading that he hadn't. What she wanted to know was whether there was going to be anything to eat tonight.

"I waited all day for a sale and, you know me, I won't come home until I've earned enough to buy us food. But it was an odd day. I'd more or less given up and was about to pack up and come home with nothing, when someone came and asked for seventy five pounds of myrrh and aloes".

"Is that so? I wonder why. That's enough for a king."

"Perhaps it was to prepare the body of Yeshua for burial," suggested Salome.

The room fell silent for a few minutes. Each of them drifted back in their minds to where they'd been during those hours of darkness. Then, from the quietness, Idris spoke, "Simeon, did you know that some people call the Pool of Siloam the 'Messiah's Pool'? Have you ever been in it"

"No, it's for people who are ill, isn't it?"

"Some people bathe in it who are not ill".

"Well, I usually walk past and go straight up to the market place," said Simeon. "Why do you ask?"

"There was a man who was born blind, who went down there and washed in the pool and came back seeing".

"What?" asked Simeon, thinking he'd misheard Idris.

"People couldn't believe it. His neighbours couldn't, even though he was standing in front of them, able to see. Those who knew he'd been born blind wondered whether it was him or somebody else who looked like him," said Idris. "All he could say was that a man who covered his eyes with mud told him to wash in the Pool of Siloam, and now he could see".

"But, even if the mud was washed from his eyes, he wouldn't be able to see because he was born blind," reasoned Simeon, "so no wonder they didn't believe it".

"You misunderstand me, Simeon," said Idris. "He could see perfectly well after washing in the pool. Everyone could see that. It was just too wonderful for them to believe. It was Yeshua who healed him. The man born blind didn't really know who he was at first. But when the scribes and Pharisees tested and cross-examined him about it, he told them that whoever it was, no-one in history had ever brought sight to someone who was born blind".

Staggered by the thought of that, Luke noticed something about what had just been said.

"If he he'd been blind all his life," reasoned Luke, "then it was not so much healing of eyes that had become poorly, but the creation of new eyes that could see".

"You're exactly right," said Idris. "So what they did was go and find his parents and vet them about their son, with questions like: is he your son, was he born blind, can he see now, did Yeshua do it?"

"It sounds like a police investigation. What did his mother and father say?" asked Luke.

"They said it was true that he was born blind".

"They could have just been saying that," said Luke, "in order to be able to prove a miracle".

"No, Luke," replied Idris. "They would have preferred not to speak to the Pharisees about the miraculous change to their son's eyes, and they certainly didn't want to speak to them about who performed the miracle".

"Why would that be?" asked Beth, puzzled by it all.

"His parents realised that what the Pharisees really wanted to know was whether they believed Yeshua was Christ, the Messiah".

"What's the difference?" asked Luke, now getting animated.

"Well, had they said Christ performed the miracle, they would have been banned from the synagogue," explained Idris, "so they told the Pharisees instead, that their son was old enough to speak for himself and that they should go and talk to him about it".

Beth tried a straightforward question, "So is Yeshua the Christ?"

Idris went quiet for a moment, composing what he had to say. "Well, the Christ, the coming one, is the one the Jews call the Messiah. People who'd seen Yeshua's miracles, were saying, 'When the Christ comes, will he do any more to show he is Christ than this man has done already?'"

9

DOOM STONE TO DAY STAR

On the morning of the first day of the week, a council was called to deal with an emergency situation. The special meeting had been convened unofficially, due to a sudden change in events in the Yeshua of Nazareth case.

Those present at the meeting included chief priests, lawyers, scribes and notable Pharisees. On the table for discussion, was the guards' report of a remarkable event having taken place at the garden tomb.

"The stone has been rolled away from the tomb," announced a chief priest for the sake of those who had not yet heard. "The soldiers tell us that the body has gone but no-one took it. None of them were injured in any way. Our thoughts are that either Yeshua's followers came secretly, whilst the guards were asleep, and took the body away to make us believe he is alive, or that the unbelievable events the guards reported, actually happened".

A lawyer began by asking: "How can we know their report is true? What grounds do you have to believe the guards?"

"We made sure that enough soldiers were guarding the tomb," said a Pharisee.

"Were the soldiers drunk?"

"They had been charged with the task of guarding the tomb," said the Pharisee. "It had been made perfectly clear to them that failure to do so would put their lives at risk. So, yes, they would have been sober".

"What if some of the guards conspired against the others, in order to allow the tomb raiders to get in?" suggested another Pharisee,

"We've thought of that possibility," replied the first Pharisee, "but it made no sense. For one, all of them would have been held responsible for failing to guard the tomb, so why do it? Also, any soldiers who'd been hoodwinked by some traitors would have the perfect excuse to escape punishment by saying that this is what happened but none of them gave this excuse. Instead, to a man, they gave us the same story of the event".

"It has to be true," declared the lawyer, "because they're sticking to an account of what happened which is the least likely to be believed. They have no motive to make up such a hard to believe story, and they cannot gain anything from it".

"It can't have happened," said a scribe.

"Let's face it. It's bad news for us if it has," said another.

"So what do we do now?" asked a chief priest.

"Keep it quiet," advised a grey-bearded elder, as he looked around for support.

"Their case is still not proven," objected another lawyer, "not until someone sees and recognises Yeshua".

"Until then, we can dismiss the few followers he still has, as madmen," suggested the lawyer.

"We have to make a choice," snapped a prominent elder. "You came for our counsel. Well my advice is to say it was a rumour, and that it was made up by deceivers who had no evidence".

A group of Pharisees whispered amongst themselves until, eventually, one said, "What will the guards say if we let them go?"

"You see to that," said a chief priest, winking at a man in the corner.

The council was about to be dismissed, when someone called out, "Wait, we can't go until we agree together another version of events".

"He's right," said the lawyer.

"Well, go on," nodded a chief priest, as he held a hand to his ear to hear what the man had to say.

"You need to invent a story for the guard and make sure every man in the guard gives exactly the same version of events. It needs to sound like the truth".

"We're saying that some followers of Yeshua came to steal the body so they could deceive people into thinking he's alive again," said the chief priest, feeling convinced in his own mind. He gave a knowing look to the man in the corner, "Take care of that, will you?"

With the business done, the whole company filed out of the shaded room in the temple into the bright sun, and marched on their way, the dust kicked up by their steps glittering momentarily as it sifted its way back to the ground.

As they stepped down into the streets of Jerusalem, they began to separate and turn round different street corners, their numbers lessening until only one was left to make his way across the market place. A few people watched him striding between the stalls. He stopped and spoke to two or three people, making no mention of the remarkable event the council had been discussing because, as far as the council were concerned, it had never happened. Singling out someone who was talking to a stallholder, he discussed something with him at length. The man nodded agreement with a council member and the two of them walked out of the market place together.

A few hundred yards from Idris' stall, a couple of side streets away, they made their way through the backstreets to where the tomb guards were being held.

The guards were mulling over their situation, and talking to each other about what they were going to say.

During the time that they had been milling around, waiting, the guards had been unable to put out of mind the things that they had seen – the hint of an angel, a blinding light as bright as lightning, the seal of the stone against the tomb entrance breaking and the huge stone rolling away.

Yet no-one had stolen the body. It was an event never witnessed before. The guards had shaken in their sandals. Now the same guards were shaking in their sandals again, at the prospect of what the council was going to do about a story that went like this: 'Something no-one has ever heard of or seen before happened and we're very sorry but the man got away'. The man, after all, was supposed to be dead.

When the council member finally walked up to them with his henchman, the guards could see they were in sombre mood.

Fixing a severe gaze upon the guards, deliberately eyeing them up one by one, so that each guard might weigh up the gravity of their situation, they came closer than the guards would have liked and scanned their faces. Without mincing words, the hired henchman spelled out clearly the terms of the business that was about to take place.

"Our arrangement with you has not gone well. It wasn't meant to turn out this way and if you don't listen carefully now, things won't turn out well for you either," he said, menacingly. "Do you understand?"

"Perfectly," answered the leader of the guard, who was inwardly considering what his options were, including making a run for it.

The go-between threatened them again, "It doesn't look good for you, now that it's come to our notice that people like you sometimes tell different stories about things that happen. Now, read my lips. You are to say that Yeshua's disciples came in the night and stole the body whilst you were asleep".

"But, that's not what happened," said the leader of the guards who, from the beginning, had felt compelled to tell the truth.

"From where I'm looking, you have no choice," said the man brokering the deal. "Yeshua disappeared on your watch. What do you think the Governor is going to do when he finds out that you've failed in your duty? Do you expect the Governor to believe stories like yours, that no-one else is prepared to believe?"

The guards looked at one another uneasily.

"I don't know why," he boomed, "you don't deserve it, but the chief priests have decided to be lenient and help you, but you also have to help us. You are to promise to stay silent about what happened. Every single one of you must promise to tell anyone who asks you, that Yeshua's followers came and stole the body. That's your side of the bargain. On our side, when this report gets to the Governor we can tell him that you did everything you could. Believe me, we can keep you out of trouble".

The guards had by now calculated that even if they wanted to say no, this was the only chance the rulers were going to give them. The leader looked around at his men for assent.

· · · · · · · · · · ●· · · · · · · · · · ·

Ariella and Atara, servants of two great houses, were talking in the market place about bits of news they'd heard about Yeshua of Galilee, from snatched whispers of conversation they'd overheard. Both belonged to wealthy households, and both were looking forward to buying something more appetising than the bitter herbs they'd procured for the table at Passover.

Idris, overhearing them, listened to what they had to say about a king who was not entertained, a crowd in a state of mass hysteria and a Roman governor who claimed not to know what truth is. They themselves had many questions and few answers.

Idris could see, by the way they were talking, that they weren't engaged in heartless gossip. He sensed an urgency in their voices. What they were saying wasn't merely matter-of-fact. They obviously cared about Yeshua. So Idris decided to stop what he was doing and listen to them. It wasn't as if he had much else to do. Trading was lax. And, just as he tuned into what they were saying, things got personal.

"Ariella, someone said that your master, Joseph of Arimathea, was going to lay Yeshua to rest in a rock-hewn tomb".

"Yes, Atara," replied Ariella, "in the tomb he had prepared for himself".

"But tell me, Ariella, if Joseph is on the Council that wanted Yeshua sentenced to death, then why would he?" Atara stared at Ariella with hardening eyes. "Is it because he was feeling guilty?"

"No!" cried Ariella, stung to the heart. "My master refused to consent to Yeshua's death when the Council met. It's the last thing he would have wanted".

Atara hadn't put it into words, but there was something about Joseph of Arimathea she didn't like. He was a wealthy man, well-respected in Jerusalem and on the Council, yet he went along with the new teaching of a poor carpenter. How could he remain in his rich man's world, acting as if nothing had happened. "He wants the best of both worlds, doesn't he?" declared Atara, dismissively.

"I've already said, he told the people around him not to do what they were doing," groaned Ariella.

"Maybe he didn't consent to Yeshua's death, but it didn't make any difference did it? We thought Yeshua was like a King to save us all, but he's dead now, isn't he?" Idris noticed the glow of tears in the corners of Atara's eyes, as she spoke.

"Joseph and Nicodemus were treating Yeshua with all the care they would a king," said Ariella, defensively. "At first, Joseph could not work out how to follow Yeshua and be who he was at the same time, but he was determined to be a disciple of Yeshua. He believed Yeshua was bringing in the Kingdom of God".

"Well, he can give up on that now. Yeshua is dead," said Atara, curtly. "Why was Yeshua condemned to death? Why has he gone from us?" she asked, forlornly. Atara was weeping now. Ariella took Atara's head to her shoulder. "I don't know why," she whispered softly.

Gently holding up Atara's head between her hands, Ariella looked into her eyes, "All I know is that other members of the Council were at rest, having completed their work as soon as the verdict was reached, but as for Joseph, his work had only just begun. He realized that now was the time to act. Joseph paid a personal visit to Pontius Pilate to ask for permission to take away the body of Yeshua". Ariella paused, remembering Yeshua so full of life, and her voice broke with tenderness as she spoke, "Joseph and Nicodemus laid the body in a new tomb in a garden".

Idris felt a tear running down his own cheek. The conversation fell silent. Idris was about to leave.

Now that they understood each other better, Atara whispered, "Did you know that kings like Manasseh and Amon and David were all buried in a garden tomb?"

"That's a sweet thought," answered Ariella. "Yes, I did".

It was bittersweet. Even Idris, a hardened trader out for what he could get, couldn't prevent the sadness that was welling up at the thought that a wonderful man who would have changed life for everyone, was gone. The only hope now, as he stood by his stall looking at the ground beneath him, was to make some sales and be able to pack up, buy some food and go home. It was business as usual but he didn't find much joy in it.

Ariella had bought what she needed from the market and was on her way back to the household, the sun's heat beading her forehead with sweat. Idris caught her eye as she walked past with her goods, "So the business of Yeshua of Nazareth is finished then," stuttered Idris.

"I think so, my master Joseph of Arimathea has rolled a huge stone against the door of the tomb. I'm afraid it's all over".

· · · · · · · · · ● · · · · · · · · · · ·

The day went somewhere. Idris could not remember much of it. Eventually, he was pre-occupied, collecting things together. What he hadn't noticed was that Beth and Luke were standing just behind him.

"Can we help?"

"Oh, it's you".

"We've been sent into the market place to find you".

"Well, here I am," he laughed.

"Any news about Yeshua and his followers?" asked Beth.

"Why do you ask that? Yeshua is not with us any more".

"I don't know. I just said it".

"His followers may have gone into hiding," he sighed. "We have no choice now, but to get on with life".

Changing tack, as he sometimes did, Luke sprung a question, "Would you be willing to help us give Simeon a surprise?"

"What are you thinking of?"

Beth and Luke explained that they needed enough wine to fill the wineskin Simeon had left lying around. They were hoping that, seeing it full again he would take a drink from it, thinking it contained water, and be in for a shock.

Idris took Beth and Luke to collect some flour and olive oil and he paid for it from the day's' earnings. He also had enough money left to help Beth and Luke with the surprise they'd planned for Simeon. When all was sorted, they headed for home.

They arrived at the house to find that Sara and Salome were not there. Simeon was alone and he looked relaxed. He'd sold all his wares.

"I think this is yours," said Idris, as he handed the old wineskin to him.

"Thank you," Simeon took a sip and looked up in surprise.

The room burst into laughter, "Is this wine for me to celebrate selling all my goods?" he wondered.

"It was just to see your face when you drank it," jabbered Luke.

When the laughter died down, Idris leaned over to Simeon and whispered, "Luke and Beth haven't said anything about the Doom Stone you told me about yet".

Simeon turned towards Luke and Beth. "I brought you here to Jerusalem in the hope you would learn about the Doom Stone clue. Have you begun to understand what it is about?"

Luke smiled uncertainly at Beth, waiting for her to say something, but instead, she returned a quick half-smile acknowledging that he could speak for them instead.

"It was behind your house that we first learned about it, especially when you told us about being trapped in the cave and what that rock you called the Doom Stone meant to some of your neighbours".

The room was dull, dusk was falling and the lamp had not yet been lit.

"I said it was an object of fear and a reason to mistrust," confessed Simeon, looking at the others with a shrug of his shoulders.

"That's because people associated it with the inevitable," replied Luke.

"Say it more simply," urged Beth.

"I'm talking about fate. The people believed you go in there and you're doomed".

"But we found out that we were not doomed to the fate they dreaded," said Beth, "because we went in and came out safely".

"And that showed us there can be hope when things look gloomy," said Luke.

"But, you have to be careful about the risks you take," advised Simeon.

"They rolled a huge stone in front of Yeshua's tomb," said Idris, remembering what Ariella had said in the market place.

"Did they?" Simeon rubbed his chin between forefinger and thumb. Then his eyes brightened, "It's a doom stone!" he said.

"Why do you call it a doom stone?" Idris wondered.

"What else is it?"

"The Doom Stone near your house had a little escape route that made it possible that we might not be trapped," Luke recalled. "But this doom stone must fully seal the entrance to Yeshua's tomb".

Idris shuddered at the thought, "So, what you're saying is that there is no escape from this doom stone".

There was no answer to that. Then Idris turned toward the door with a troubled look on his face, as though he had been reminded of something. Instantly, Luke and Beth had read it. It was a look of concern. He was worried about Sara.

Beth and Luke rose up immediately and walked to the door, in search of Sara and Salome. Behind them, as they stepped out into the street, they could hear Idris saying to Simeon, "I don't know where Sara and Salome are. They should be back by now".

Luke and Beth stayed on the street, watching out for Salome and Sara. The dusk had long since turned into night. As they stood by the door, nothing seemed right. They still couldn't guess where the clues were leading them. So what had the stranger in the desert been trying to tell them? Right now, though, they needed to think about Idris. Idris had helped them with their clue. But now it was time to think about the help he needed.

Where were Sara and Salome? They were always there in the house to meet them when Luke and Beth had been out in Jerusalem. What had happened to them? The least they could do for Idris was to try and find Sara and Salome, but which street were they to turn down? Sara and Salome could be anywhere this side of the Temple.

"You run that way and I'll run this way". Beth was already running as she said it.

Luke yelled after Beth, "And we'll meet back here in ten minutes!" as Beth disappeared into the night.

He stood still a moment and tried to think clearly. He thought they may have been to the market to help Idris buy the food for tonight.

"I know", he whispered to himself, "what must have happened is that they'll have just missed us, because they prefer going up the steps to get to the market". With that in mind, Luke sprinted for the steps.

Runnels of sweat trickling slowly through Beth's hair were starting to pour down her temples, as she swung round another corner. The streets all looked the same to her and, although she ran on, she started to realise she may be lost.

Ahead, on the corner at the next crossroads, she could see a figure crouched down. Was he waiting to pounce on her? Beth slowed her pace to a walk, but that made her feel even more nervous. It seemed an age before she was about to pass the figure. Should she act normal or start running away?

Just then, two people turned the corner and in moments she could see it was Salome and Sara. She'd never been so relieved to see them.

"Who' was that on the corner of the street?" she asked when they were a safe distance away.

"That's a beggar," said Sara. Although Sara was perfectly calm, there was something thin and fragile about the way she spoke.

"Are you all right, Sara?"

"A little overwhelmed, you'll forgive me," Sara replied, "but Salome and I have heard something we thought was impossible".

Instead of asking what it was, Beth was more intent on putting distance between her and the beggar. So she was surprised when Salome said, "Wait here while I go back to give this beggar a mite".

She watched as Salome walked over to him, handed him a mite and stopped to tell him something. He looked up and, after a while, smiled with delight, as if he were receiving something more than money.

"What was it you heard?" asked Beth, when Salome returned.

"We heard that Yeshua is alive," marvelled Salome.

"So you told the beggar," said Beth.

"I just have to tell everyone. It's such a wonderful thing that's happened".

"It's true," said Sara, "we can hardly believe it".

When they reached the door of the house, they found Luke standing there waiting for them. "Let's go in," said Sara.

Idris was happy yet bewildered, as he stood up, seeing at once that Sara and Salome were shaken. Instead of saying 'where've you been?' he spoke more gently, "What is it, Sara?"

Sara announced, "Yeshua is alive!" as surprised as she was when she first heard the news.

"What?" asked Simeon. "How can this be?"

"We were climbing up the steps from the Tyropoeon valley, on our way to the market when we heard a voice call 'Salome!' So we stopped, thinking that someone wanted to talk to Salome, but it was another Salome," said Sara. "I don't think they knew we were there".

"What did you hear?" Simeon tried to hurry them along, but Salome asked if she could sit down first, so Sara, acting as hostess, made her comfortable then sat down beside her and started to explain.

"Well, when Salome, the other Salome, turned round there was such a beautiful smile on her face. She was telling her friend that on the day after the Sabbath, as they carried spices to the garden tomb to anoint Yeshua's body, they'd been asking each other whether they'd be able to move the large stone away from the entrance to the garden tomb. Then when they arrived there, they found that it had been rolled aside".

Luke looked at Beth: "So the doom stone was moved".

"It wasn't a doom stone. It was only a stone," answered Beth, and all the heaviness they'd felt about the stone disappeared.

"Let's establish the facts then," said Luke. "Are we sure the stone was actually rolled in front of the tomb in the first place?"

"I heard that Mary Magdalene and the other Mary were there at the time. They sat down opposite the tomb, after the stone was rolled in front of it" said Salome.

"So that's one fact," said Luke.

"There's more. Mary Magdalene was crying as she came to the tomb," said Sara, "but when she looked inside she saw two angels, one where his head had been and one where his feet had been".

"That's unbelievable," said Luke.

"Yet it's true," said Salome. "because they asked her, 'Woman, why are you weeping?'".

"She said, 'Because they have taken away my Lord'," continued Sara. "Then Yeshua was standing there, and he asked, 'Woman, why are you weeping? Whom are you seeking?' but she thought at first that he was the gardener".

"Then when he said, 'Mary', she realised it was Yeshua and that he was alive again," said Sara.

"Yeshua is alive," said Salome.

Over the evening meal, everyone had plenty to say, but nobody knew what to think. All six went out on to the street afterwards and looked up at the star-speckled sky.

"The stars shine brightly tonight," said Idris. "I cannot tell whether it's because I am happy or because they are brighter".

"All those thousands of stars are bright, but the day star is by far the brightest," Salome's eyes twinkled, perhaps with something more than the reflection of the stars. "Light that is too bright to look upon has come in the man Yeshua," she said.

Everyone walked inside, except Beth. She simply stood there, saying to herself, "Day Star, Day Star," until Ben came out, grabbed her by the arm and pulled her in, "You have to be careful not to be alone at night", he said.

She remembered how she'd run alone in the dark, through the streets of Jerusalem. "Tell me about it!" she said, not expecting a reply. Then she thought about the beggar. Would he get any sleep on the hard ground tonight?

10

THE OUTSIDERS STAY IN

Climbing the steps up to the market place, Salome remembered to say, "We must be careful to get back early, or Idris will worry about you".

"Yes," agreed Sara, "but so many things have happened this last week, who knows what's going to happen next".

"Where's Idris today?"

"He went to the market place to start with, then he's going over to the Temple Mount".

When Sara and Salome reached Idris' stall, there he was, looking embarrassed, talking to two women.

"This is Atara and Ariella," he said, "I met them when they were upset the other day," and turning to Ariella and Atara, "This is my wife Sara and her cousin Salome".

"Shalom," smiled Atara and Ariella.

Salome could see an ease, not just a freedom from drudgery but a positive joy in them.

"Atara and Ariella say that more people have heard Yeshua is alive," reported Idris.

"Yes," said Ariella. "Not only has Mary Magdalene seen Yeshua alive but an angel of the Lord told Joanna and Mary the mother of James and the other women that Yeshua is risen".

"Is it only women who have seen and heard that Yeshua is alive?" asked Sara.

"When Mary Magdalene went to tell the men the tomb was empty, it seemed like hearsay to them, but Peter ran to see, in the hope it might be true," said Atara. "Another disciple ran with him and reached the tomb first and found it empty. Then Yeshua came that evening and stood in the midst of his disciples and said, 'Peace be with you'".

While the women gossiped the latest news, standing in the market place, Idris was feeling happier about trading. In some ways it was a day like any day, but now there was a freshness and newness in the air.

The news that Yeshua was alive was almost impossible to believe, but it was being confirmed by fresh sightings. Rising from the dead was something completely new, thought Idris. No-one had ever heard of it happening in what Luke and Beth called BC.

Idris restrained himself from talking with Ariella and Atara about Luke and Beth's clue, because he knew there was no way he could tell them that two visitors from two thousand years' time, happened to be staying at his house.

In the large households in which they worked, Ariella and Atara were well-accustomed to spreading out and folding up cloths of various kinds. It was part of their daily routine. Perhaps that was why one detail they'd learnt about the empty tomb, had caught their attention.

"It puzzled me," said Atara, "that inside the empty tomb, a cloth that was wrapped around Yeshua's head, had been folded up and put in another place, away from where his head had lain. The strips of linen from around his body had been cast aside, but this cloth had been folded up on purpose".

After Ariella and Atara had left, Sara and Salome were talking about this interesting fact and what it meant, as they walked around the market, buying provisions for the day. Sara's neighbour, Hannah, who was in the market place, heard them speaking about Yeshua, as they were about to leave. She greeted Sara and Salome, and as she was on her way home too, all three walked together down the steps.

"Did you hear that the stone blocking Yeshua's tomb entrance was rolled aside?" said Hannah, as they walked down between the stone walls.

"Yes, and that Yeshua is alive too," said Sara, still flush with fresh news of him.

"I think someone must have stolen the body," said Hannah, striking a different tone.

"Why would anyone want to steal the body?" asked Salome.

"To prove Yeshua was alive, I would think," said Hannah, sceptically.

"And how would that be possible with a dead body?" Salome's eyes caught Hannah's eyes and held them. "Think about it, Hannah".

"Just because you don't know why they did it, doesn't mean they didn't do it".

"If they had overpowered the soldiers who were guarding the tomb and taken the body, would they want to linger at the tomb or disappear quickly into the night?" Salome's eyes sparkled with the question.

"They'd run off quickly, of course," said Hannah, surprised she'd been asked. "Why do you ask?"

"Because in the empty tomb, a grave cloth that had been wrapped around Yeshua's head was left folded up and laid in a separate place from the strips of linen".

It sounded inconsequential at first. Hannah pondered the fact for a moment and said, "Why would they do that?"

"Yes, why would they do that?" repeated Salome.

"I can't really think of a reason," Hannah's eyes searched for an explanation. "Anyway," she sighed, "it's the last thing they'd do if they were in a hurry".

"You've got it!" shrieked Sara.

"What am I not understanding?" asked Hannah.

"Only that the only person who would have done that was Yeshua himself," said Sara, leaving Hannah staring at the obvious.

"But Yeshua would have to be alive to do that!" said Hannah, hardly daring to imagine what it meant. "Oh, I see what you mean".

Hannah said goodbye to Sara and Salome at the door. "She's a nice neighbour," said Salome, as soon as they were in the house.

"It felt like somebody had got to her already. Don't you sense some people are deliberately selling the line that the body of Yeshua has been stolen?" said Sara.

As Sara and Salome settled down to the housework, a quietness took over, a space in which they could have their own thoughts, but it wasn't long before they were talking again.

"Simeon's got itchy feet," Salome confided to Sara. "He's sold all his cloths, spices, pots and perfumes, and," with a knowing sideways glance at Sara, she said, "he's been dropping hints that it's time to go".

"It's been so good to spend some time with you," said Sara. "Silly me, I'd got so used to having you both here". Sara caught her breath as her eyes misted, "Can't you persuade him to stay?"

"I've tried, but he's adamant that he needs to go back to get more stock from the desert traders".

"Of course, he must," reflected Sara, "but Luke and Beth need to stay and solve the puzzle that'll help them return to their own time." She blinked, wondering what on earth she was speaking about.

"Yes, they will need to stay," agreed Salome. "Would it be all right for them to stay here until Simeon and I return with more goods?"

"We'd love to have them stay".

"As long as Idris doesn't mind".

"He won't. He'll probably be asking them to help sell his spices in Jerusalem," Sara paused. "I'm surprised Idris hasn't recruited Simeon already".

"Mind you, Simeon will miss Beth and Luke".

"Idris and Simeon have been quite taken by the two strangers from distant time".

"What you mean is they're coping well with two people from the future currently following the throwaway instructions of an unknown man they briefly met in the wilderness just over a week ago," concluded Salome, and they both burst into laughter.

Simeon longed to help Beth and Luke with their quest, but if he wanted success in the marketplace, he knew it was up to him to go home and get hold of goods at a cheaper price than he would be required to pay in Jerusalem.

Yet, Simeon was convinced that the message for the modern world that Luke and Beth would take to their own time, was far more important than an argument with a desert herdsman about the price of a pot. So, for the time being, he intended to stay around until the way ahead was clear.

But it wasn't easy for him. Simeon had been aimlessly walking the streets, trying to work out what to do. He'd returned to the house and was sitting at the door brooding, when Idris came back from the market bazaar and almost fell over him in the doorway. "Mind who you're treading on," grunted Simeon.

Idris looked at him brightly, "Would you like to earn some money selling spices with me by the Temple?"

"Yes, I would like that very much. Thank you for asking," Simeon leapt at the opportunity and soon they were discussing the best way to sell.

Idris hoped that between the two of them, they'd make more sales by the Temple Mount, but Simeon thought differently. Though he was happy to come along and see what was going on, he was sure he'd sell much more if Idris and he were selling in two different places.

Simeon had been nursing a plan to sell at an unusual spot he'd noticed not far from the market place, where many of the people had more money to spend and less time to spend it.

· · · · · · · · · ● · · · · · · · · · · ·

Idris and Simeon left the house not long after dawn. Jerusalem was awakening, and the hum of life was in its streets.

The morning went slowly for Sara and Salome, who were washing and cleaning the house. Meanwhile, Beth and Luke slipped out to run around and play.

"Where are Luke and Beth?" asked Salome.

"They usually go down by the South Gate to play, then on to the Pool of Siloam. I think they'll probably be by the Pool now," replied Sara. "They've started going down there to dip their feet in the water".

"I can understand that. It's hot today, are you going up to the market place when it's cooler," asked Salome.

"Yes, I think so. Would you like to come with me?"

"Yes, I'll collect Beth and Luke from beside the Pool, and we can all go up together".

Luke and Beth were down at the South Gate of Jerusalem, playing one of their favourite games. They had a name for it - Jerusalem Cricket. In this game they stood on either side of the thoroughfare and one counted the number of animal legs going in and one counted the number of animal legs going out through the gate of Jerusalem for about half an hour. They scored each leg as a run. Their imaginary teams were the 'Insiders' (counting going in) and the 'Outsiders' (counting going out).

The Outsiders usually won. Luke thought he knew why the results were like that. He hadn't wanted to mention it to Beth so he could win a bet with her. But when it became too obvious the Outsiders would win, he gave up the idea of making a bet. That was, until it occurred to him that they played the game in the morning and that after midday more people and supplies would be likely to be arriving from distant towns. For this reason, he felt that the Insiders were bound to win in the afternoons. By going to the Pool of Siloam first, Luke had engineered things so that they would play the game in the afternoon.

"I bet the Insiders win," yelled Luke across the gateway as all the people bustled past.

"No chance, Luke, the Outsiders always win".

"OK, I bet you the Insiders win and if they don't, then you owe me a week's allowance when we get back to the twenty first century".

Beth smiled, "Deal!" as she caught sight of a tethered goat nearby, hoping it was about to be taken out through the gate.

Sure enough, more and more sheep, goats and beasts of burden were being led into Jerusalem. It didn't take Beth long to see why.

"These animals are very dusty, Luke," she said.

"That's true," Luke's smug tone indicated to Beth that something funny was going on.

"You know why, don't you?" Beth knew he was hiding something. Then it came to her, "The animals are so dusty because they've come from a long way away and you knew the people and goods from faraway towns and villages would be bound to arrive in the afternoon, didn't you?"

"Well, yes," he replied, as a kind of apology for his greatness.

"That was mean of you, Luke. It wasn't chance. You calculated you could make money out of me, without telling me about it".

Luke cracked. "I'm sorry, Beth". The secret stratagem he'd employed to make money out of the situation seemed second-rate now. "I'm so sorry. I just wanted to make some money".

"And forget about your best friend".

"I suppose that laying bets can make you greedy for more and more, if you're not careful," he admitted.

"So, let's not bet any more," was Beth's solution.

"OK, let's score points instead. Look, Beth, I'm really sorry I did that".

"It's all right. I might have done the same".

"But, you didn't".

"No".

Higher up the Tyropoeon Valley, behind them, a heat haze hung over the city of Jerusalem.

Idris was trading by the Temple. Simeon was standing still next to him. He felt a bit awkward, but he wasn't going to say anything. Instead, he waited to see if Idris would take up his idea of separating, but it didn't look like it was going to happen any time soon.

Simeon watched Idris serve the occasional customer, for more than an hour, then turned to him and asked Idris politely, if he might allow him to take some of the spices and sell them by the marketplace. To his surprise, Idris said, "I was wondering when you were going to ask me that".

Idris asked a friend at the Temple Mount, to lend Simeon a donkey. Then he asked Simeon to return home and load as many spices as possible on to the donkey.

As soon as he saw the animal, Simeon ran to grasp hold of the donkey. He pulled the donkey along at a trot, and was home in no time. He went on the understanding that Idris himself would come down later to retrieve the donkey and return it to its owner.

Simeon was making his way to the market place after loading, when a child with a hoop came skidding down a side street and collided with the donkey. Simeon stretched forward just in time and caught the load before it toppled to the ground. Sweating with the strain, he looked up to chide the boy, but the child was nowhere to be seen.

Reaching the marketplace, Simeon walked the donkey past all the tables and set up stall against the fortified walls next to the entrance to Herod's Palace. He was standing right in the face of the Romans and the Royal household who pass through there. No-one had ever dared take up a pitch so close to the palace entrance before.

When Idris came across for the donkey, later in the afternoon, he was surprised to see how many customers Simeon had. In the short time Idris had been there,

Simeon had served more customers than Idris was used to serving in an entire morning. He felt the need to compliment Simeon.

"You're a brave man to set your stall up here, Simeon," he said, waving in the direction of the imposing perimeters of Herod's Palace. "It looks like you're selling more than I ever do. I've brought you the rest of the spices here".

"Thank you," whispered Simeon as he was dealing with a customer.

"Hasn't anyone asked you what you're doing here right outside the palace?" asked Idris.

"No-one has tried to move me on yet," replied Simeon, with a cheeky smile. "For some reason, people from the palace seem pleased I'm here and keen to buy the spices. They've got the money to pay for them too," he winked.

"Spices are bound to brighten up the food and smell of a palace!" laughed Idris. "Shall I stay and see if I can help you".

"Why not?"

After Idris joined Simeon, more and more people started coming up from the market to see what was happening. As the crowd grew, even more people were attracted to the spot and, before long Simeon and Idris were both busy selling non-stop.

169

Idris hardly had time to think, but then idly noticing the donkey he suddenly remembered why he'd come. He pointed at the animal and said, "I need to go!"

Idris loaded everything on to the donkey, except the remaining spices, which he laid on a cloth on the ground.

Coming out from the market place, Idris met Salome who, with Beth and Luke, had been searching for Simeon.

"Everyone's gone missing today. I was supposed to meet Sara here earlier on," said Salome, "but I was late because Beth and Luke weren't where I expected them to be. Sara must have moved on and I couldn't find Simeon by the Temple Mount, either".

"Simeon is here, but you won't be able to spot him among the other traders, because he's by the gates of Herod's Palace".

"What? Next to the gates, did you say?"

"Yes, right outside the gates," spluttered Idris.

"Thank you, where did you get the donkey from, by the way?"

"A friend lent it to me".

Salome knew there was a story there but she wasn't going to ask about it. She thought Sara might have something to say if the little money they had was going on a donkey, but Idris guessed what she was thinking. "Don't worry," he said. "My friend's not charging for it".

Luke and Beth couldn't believe their eyes when they saw the queue that was mounting up by the palace gates for Simeon's spices. He barely had a moment to greet them.

Beth laughed and she nudged Beth, "Do you remember when we first met Simeon, he was roaming the wilderness trying to sell one simlah?"

"Yes, he couldn't sell a sun shade on a boiling hot day in the desert," laughed Luke. "They must like him here in Jerusalem".

Looking around, Salome sensed there was a slightly edgy atmosphere. Few were staying to argue the price and sales were going quickly, too quickly, as if they felt they shouldn't be there. She noticed that the guards on sentry duty by the gate, looked nervous as they eyed the pressing crowd.

The sentries knew that any blockage to movement in or out of the palace meant trouble for them. They had sent word to the centurion in charge of the guard at the Praetorium. The centurion received the message and applied for permission to take out a detachment to see what the problem was.

Looking back at the market place, Beth caught a glimpse of Sara and ran towards her, but Sara hadn't noticed and moved away. Beth was out of breath by the time she finally caught up with her.

"Sara, sorry we didn't meet you".

"I wondered where you were, and where's Salome?".

"She's over there. I'm sorry, Luke and I held her up".

"Never mind, we've found each other now".

When Sara joined the others, she brought more news of Yeshua. Turning toward the crowded market place, she pointed, "That's Salome, the woman who said Yeshua is alive. It was one of her friends who told me".

"Told you what?" asked Salome.

At that moment, Roman troops turned the corner, each soldier with a *gladius* in hand. At their head a centurion was marching towards Simeon. As the soldiers drew near, they gripped their weapons more tightly and steeled themselves for what was to come. The centurion hurled his sword into the ground next to Simeon, who spun round and looked up in disbelief. It was Justinus.

"So it's you causing all this commotion!"

To everyone's surprise, Justinus took off his helmet, placed it in the small of his arm, and slapped the left side of his chest with a deep sense of honour. Simeon was staring at a Roman centurion in full regalia, his armour shining in the golden sunlight of late afternoon.

"Justinus, what can I say? It's a pleasure to see you again," beamed Simeon, his face full of perspiration.

"I thought we were coming to crush a rebellion but it turned out to be you".

"I'm just selling a few spices, as you can see".

"It looks like you're having a good day", returned the centurion, with no hint that he was about to spoil it. "Jerusalem hasn't done you any harm then," said Justinus, glancing at the bulge in Simeon's money bag.

"I love Jerusalem, Do you like it, Justinus?"

"We've been too busy to see much of Jerusalem. The troop will be returning to Galilee this week". Justinus wasn't speaking hand over mouth as if divulging secret information, but openly, as to a friend. So openly, that Salome felt confident enough to step up with the news she was bursting to tell.

"I've been told Yeshua will be in Galilee to see his disciples by the Sea of Tiberius," she announced, being careful to use the Roman name for the lake.

"Please can we go and see him there!" shouted Beth, embarrassing her brother somewhat. She looked imploringly at Justinus. "Can we go up to Galilee with you?"

"You can come with us if you're willing to help carry our baggage," said the Roman centurion invitingly. "What do you say, Simeon?"

"You remembered my name".

"How could I forget it? And you remembered mine." Then, trying not to be too familiar, he caught the eye of his men and sternly declared in a louder voice: "Do you want to be arrested or are you going to leave quietly?"

"Don't worry, we'll go quietly," replied Simeon.

Justinus looked into Simeon's face and, with little more than a whisper, told him, "Be here this time tomorrow, if you'd like to come with us".

"We'll either be here or, if we're not, we wish you a safe journey in advance," said Simeon, quietly.

"Agreed," Justinus turned, marshalled his men and marched them off to the Praetorium.

Instantly, Simeon was dreaming of new opportunities to sell goods in Galilee. He was imagining the journey as a fact-finding visit to discover what items the people were short of and then, having learnt the route there, he planned to return again with wares from the south to meet demand.

Beth turned to Simeon, "So we're going to Galilee?"

"It looks like it," said Simeon.

"I'll come too," smiled Salome. She knew Simeon's main aim would be to find a new market for his goods but, like him, she yearned for Beth and Luke to find their way home.

"We're on the trail!" whooped Beth.

Simeon was walking around like an entrepreneur who'd got it made, with doors to vast markets opening up to him. "It's time my donkey came back into commission," he smiled. "She'll be strong enough for the journey by now".

"I could borrow my friend's donkey and come along too," said Idris, hopefully. But, Sara made it transparently clear she would not be able to hold house and home together without him, and so Idris had to concede that it made perfect sense for him to stay at home in Jerusalem.

It was obvious what to do, as far as Sara was concerned. Simeon and Salome would go up through Samaria to Galilee, then circle round past the lake, down along the Jordan valley and back up to Jerusalem from Jericho. Luke and Beth would meet Yeshua in Galilee and complete the puzzle that would enable them to return to their own century. But when Sara looked at Idris, she could see how much he wanted to go and her heart melted.

"Now I think of it," she said, "we have those big spools of wool the shepherds left us when they took some of your spices last year. I can make enough money spinning them, as long as you come straight back from Galilee, Idris".

"I shall," muttered Idris. Then he turned to the others and said, "Looks like I'll be having fish for breakfast with you in Galilee, after all!"

"And just in case Luke and Beth are not successful, they can come back here with you," suggested Salome.

"Thank you for that, Salome," sighed a relieved looking Luke, "I'm glad someone had thought about it".

"She does think about people," said Simeon who, having heard her name, was at last, paying attention to what was being said. "She thinks about everyone".

"Well, I do try," said Salome, modestly.

"Yeshua cared for everybody," said Idris. Salome's eyes met his, in agreement. "He made the outsiders feel that they were in, and they started to trust in him".

Simeon said, "We heard that Yeshua went up on a mountain, and a crowd listened to him and that he spoke about loving your enemies, blessing those who curse you, and doing good to those who hate you," Simeon leant his head to one side and screwed his eyes up, quizzically. "How can you bless your enemies when they do you wrong?"

Idris' face brightened, "I do not think he meant you to bless the wrong they do, but, instead, to bless them by doing good to them".

11

FISH FOR BREAKFAST

"Fish for breakfast! Wake up, Beth and Luke! We're having fish for breakfast! Wake up!"

Beth and Luke bounded downstairs to find the table all set for breakfast. Normally, they would come downstairs when they felt like it on a Saturday, and expect to sort out their own breakfast from what they could find in the kitchen. But this Saturday morning was different.

"I've been shouting for ages," moaned Dad. "Come on, Mum's cooked fish for breakfast".

"I've just been dreaming about fish for breakfast," mumbled Beth, as she began to eat.

"My dream was about fish for breakfast too!" shouted Luke, his eyes opening wide.

"It's kedgeree actually," said Mum, quietly.

"What?"

"The breakfast".

"Whatever it is, it looks a mess, Mum," said Beth, gazing down at the plate. She turned to her brother with a look of astonishment on her face, "How unlikely is that? We had the same dream!"

"REM sleep can happen very quickly, so you may have heard me shouting 'fish for breakfast' and both dreamt about it," explained Dad.

"What's REM sleep?" asked Beth.

"It's when you are sleeping and your eyes are twitching," said Luke, butting in before Dad could answer. "It's called Rapid Eye Movement and that happens when you're dreaming".

Beth laughed, "Mine was funny. We met a kind man in the desert and then tumbled down a slope of sand and he had to shake the sand out of his beard!"

"What happened then?" asked Mum, bemused.

"The man gave us two clues," replied Beth. "One was BC and Luke said Fred had told him what it meant".

"Fred?" asked Luke.

"You know, your teacher Fred".

"That Fred?"

"Never mind which Fred," Dad interrupted. "You need to eat up, you've got a long journey ahead of you".

"Where are we going?" murmured Luke, as he slurped his last mouthful of kedgeree.

"Somewhere with Auntie Shona and Uncle Doyle," said Mum.

"It's a secret," said Dad.

"Brilliant! We like Auntie Shona and Uncle Doyle," enthused Luke.

"Auntie Shona used to cook us millionaire's shortbread and sing us to sleep," remembered Beth, "and Uncle Doyle makes us laugh".

"You'll have to pass, on the millionaire's shortbread this time," announced Dad, "you're going to be eating different food".

"So where are we going?" asked Luke.

"Here you are," replied Dad, roughly handing over hiking boots and sun screen. "These are the best clues I'm going to give you".

"Auntie Shona and Uncle Doyle will tell you where you're going. It's a surprise," said Mum. "Now go and put your things in the suitcases I've put out for you," she whispered.

"What things shall we take?" asked Beth.

They're all ironed and neatly folded next to the suitcases. You won't need to bring much else".

"I hope you've included Octopus and Big Ted," squawked Beth.

"No, you can bring Squirrel and Mouse instead. That's my final offer".

"But Luke doesn't even play with Mouse any more," whined Beth, and she stomped out of the room.

Luke didn't want to leave Mouse behind, and Big Ted went with him everywhere, he couldn't leave Big Ted behind. It took a lot of arguing until at last Mum conceded. Somehow they managed to squeeze Big Ted in under the lid.

"That's it," Mum gave a sigh of relief. "Big Ted and Squirrel packed for the holiday!"

"Do you remember Beth before the holiday in Cornwall," said Dad. "She was only three and she told us she'd packed Squirrel for the holiday".

"When we asked her if she'd packed Squirrel for the holiday, she said 'Yes'," laughed Mum, "but she left Squirrel in her suitcase all holiday, because she'd said: 'Squirrel is packed for the holiday!'"

· · · · · · · · ● · · · · · · · · · · ·

Unbeknown to Beth and Luke, Shona and Doyle had been going through a crisis in their marriage. Both were hoping that the holiday might be as much a tonic to their marriage as it would be a surprise to Beth and Luke.

The crisis came to a head with an unexpected change of circumstances. Doyle's job at a chocolate factory in Somerset was taken away from him, when a big foreign company took over the firm. Before it bought out the old company and all its factories, the new company promised to save all the jobs of the workers at the Somerset site, but as soon as it took over it sacked everyone there.

Doyle was left wondering what there was that he could trust. He felt he could trust Shona. Perhaps he could trust his bank manager, but before long there'd be nothing in the bank to trust him with except how to manage an overdraft.

Hoping he was in between jobs, Doyle found himself at a loss as to what to do. In the end, he chose to lounge around at home. This was not good news for Shona, who was learning to get by with less money but finding it hard to put up with the one she hoped would be a solution to the problem now becoming a problem, making the place untidy and getting in the way of her usual household routine.

Shona was a qualified pharmacologist. They'd met when she was a student and he was taking a boiler out at her hall of residence. She stopped for a chat. He invited her out for fish and chips on his lunch break and the rest is history.

After Doyle had lost his job, Shona took on more hours at the chemists. At home, they had arguments about the way they saw the situation and a barrier formed between them. She went to church every Sunday and he went to the pub, and she met him there afterwards, but often they didn't talk.

It was tempting for Shona to picture Doyle as a weak individual without enough imagination to do any more than mope around at home, but she held on to the hope that he would get out more and maybe find a job. In spite of the fact they'd argued about it, secretly Doyle agreed with Shona's advice that he should get out of the house and do something. Perhaps he could get away to the country. He loved mountains but there weren't any in Somerset. In the end, he decided to go for a walk up Glastonbury Tor, in order to clear his head.

The weather was changing for the worse as he arrived in Glastonbury. He walked up to the top of Glastonbury's High Street, then out past Wick Hollow and along Stone Down lane to the far side of the Tor. Climbing the steep steps, he pitted himself against wind and driving rain, until he came out on the top of the hill.

The sky was dark and bleak, but over in the distance a washed-out light was beginning to gleam over the Somerset Levels. Doyle decided to shelter from the rain under the stone tower that is all that remains of St Michael's church on the tor's summit.

Looking past the windswept, rain-lashed stone wall of the tower, Doyle remembered the Celtic crosses he'd visited in Ireland. He recalled one somewhere, which depicted two snakes locked together, destroying each other on the face of the cross.

Gazing at the stonework of the tower, he felt like an archaeologist and smiled wryly as a thought came to mind: 'I'm an archaeologist - my career is in ruins!'

The weather had brightened so Doyle thought he'd pay his first visit to Glastonbury Abbey. He liked the story of the Knights of the Round Table. He'd heard that King Arthur and Queen Guinevere's tomb and the tomb of Joseph of Arimathea were there.

Before visiting the place, Doyle spent a short time in each of a number of bookshops in the town, reading up all he could about King Arthur and Joseph of Arimathea.

He treated himself to lunch in a Glastonbury café, then took himself around Glastonbury Abbey.

Whilst admiring a patch of fresco decoration on the wall of the Lady's Chapel, he heard a guide speaking about Joseph of Arimathea, whose tomb was visible down on the floor below. Doyle looked at the tomb, wondering if it was really true that Joseph had been buried there.

The guide said, "The bible says Joseph of Arimathea was Jesus' uncle".

When Doyle arrived home, he pulled out a copy of the New Testament his parents had given him, which he'd never bothered to read, and pored over it. When Shona came home from work, she was pleased to see him doing something other than watching television.

The next day Doyle read the New Testament all the way through, and found that nowhere did it say that Joseph of Arimathea was Jesus' uncle. He began to wonder whether sometimes people think the bible says things that it doesn't actually say.

He pressed his fingertips against his forehead, and tried to think of a well-known saying from the bible. The first to come to mind was: "Money is the root of all evil".

Doyle picked up his phone and tapped the words in, only to find that it doesn't really say that, but what it does say, is: "The love of money is the root of all evil". 'Interesting', he thought, 'I didn't know that, even though I must have already read that today'. Then he slumped back on the couch and fell asleep.

When Shona returned from work, seeing him lying there, she muttered to herself, "Looks like he's back to normal".

· · · · · · ●●●●● ● ●●●●● · · · · · ·

Beth liked getting organised, and to be organised she needed to know what she was doing and where she was going, so she kept on asking where Auntie Shona and Uncle Doyle would to be taking them, but Mum and Dad weren't giving anything away.

Beth and Luke were waiting at the gate when Shona and Doyle finally arrived. Doyle opened the car door and their adventure began.

As Shona drove the car away, Doyle turned round from the passenger seat and said, "Next stop Kathmandu!"

"Where?" asked Beth.

"Kathmandu," answered Shona, as she focussed on the road.

Luke vaguely recalled having heard the name. "Where is it?" he asked.

"It's near India, in a country called Nepal," replied Doyle.

Luke grinned, "So that's why we had all those injections".

"I think…I'm sure there were only two," wavered Doyle.

"There were more than two," countered Beth.

"Whatever it was," said Shona, "I'm sure it's going to be worth it".

It was not long before Luke and Beth were online, trying to find out about Kathmandu and Nepal. Then, after negotiating Heath Row airport, some films, some music, some meals, some sleeps, another airport and some half-sleep, they were touching down in Kathmandu, which was quite different from landing at Paris Charles de Gaulle airport, Luke and Beth's only other airport destination.

"It's been a long journey," said Beth, wearily, as they waited for the luggage.

"That's because it's a long way," said Shona.

"Yes, we had the long flight to Delhi first," sympathised Doyle. "Then changing flights and flying here took a long time. How are you feeling, Luke?"

"I'm looking forward to exploring Kathmandu," he replied, stretching his arms out with a yawn, "and I want to do some mountain biking".

"We're meeting some friends here. Do you remember Dhonu and Amisha, who were staying with us one time when you came for a holiday?" asked Shona. Luke and Beth's expressions remained neutral.

"They live here and they're going to show you around," said Doyle.

"You say they'll be showing us around. What will you be doing?" asked Beth.

"Ahh... Auntie Shona and I have something to do," replied Doyle, as he took possession of the suitcases.

"Have we?" asked Shona.

"I thought we needed some time together, just the two of us".

"Where are we going?"

"Into the mountains," replied Doyle, walking away.

"So you're going to dump us!" screeched Beth, running alongside.

Doyle stopped walking and looked at Beth. "I'm not sure we'll be doing that". He swallowed hard and paused to think. "You know, Dhonu and Amisha have already met you and you'll enjoy playing with their son Aashish".

"Look, they're here!" cried Shona.

"Welcome to Kathmandu," said Dhonu, with a big smile, as he picked up one of the suitcases.

"Have you had a good journey?" asked Amisha.

"I did until Uncle Doyle and Auntie Shona told us they're going away for a while," said Beth, pushing back the tears.

"Oh, are they?" replied Amisha, looking up at them, with a question in her eyes.

"We just needed to get away for a couple of days," explained Doyle. "Is that OK, Amisha?"

"I'm sure it'll be all right won't it, Dhonu?"

"Not a problem".

"Where are you going?" demanded Beth.

"To Namche Bazaar, to see Everest".

"Please can we come with you?" pleaded Beth.

"Young people are more in danger of altitude sickness," said Dhonu, sensibly. "It'll be too high for you up there".

"So when do you leave?" asked Amisha.

"Tomorrow," said Doyle, looking at Shona, in the hope that she understood why he'd booked the seats.

"Good, so you can come back and have something to eat with us now," said Dhonu.

When they arrived back at the house, Beth and Luke met Aashish who was home from school.

"I should have finished my homework soon," said Aashish, "and then we can go out and play".

"Cheer up, Beth. We'll enjoy it," said Luke. "We'd only get altitude sickness if we went up the mountains with Auntie Shona and Uncle Doyle".

Upstairs. Shona and Doyle unpacked their suitcases and squeezed their outdoor gear into rucksacks, ready for their trip to Namche Bazaar.

· · · · · · · · ● · · · · · · · · · ·

It was on the flight to Lukla, that Shona realised she was going to get more than she bargained for, especially when Lukla's runway came into sight. It was the shortest she'd ever seen, with no margin for error, set in the middle of precipitous mountains. She was petrified, but told herself the pilot knew what he was doing. After a white knuckle landing, Doyle was given a hard time as Shona told him just what she thought about his having booked her on that flight.

Shona looked around at the mountains, wondering how steep the slopes would be on the mountain trek Doyle had promised her out of Namche Bazaar.

As the helicopter to Namche wheeled away from Lukla, snow-covered peaks came into sight. Sweeping through a deep valley, between steep, rocky slopes, gaping forest-clad gorges came into sight where waterfalls scored threaded white lines down mountainsides.

The helicopter tore through the sky toward Namche Bazaar. As it dipped to land, opening her eyes, Shona was immediately aware of the steepness of the drop from the rim of stones around the helipad, down to the houses below

"That was breath-taking," said Doyle.

"I don't know, I wasn't looking," answered Shona, wondering how exposed it was going to feel, stepping on to the stones.

Scooping up their rucksacks, they clambered out of the helicopter, and quickly moved aside. Almost as soon as it had come, the helicopter peeled away and swung noisily into the distance, whilst on the stone apron its two passengers stood dazed, looking at the view.

Sharp, silhouetted peaks gave way to higher sharp peaks, from which rose a large mountain mass, dusted with snow. Further in the distance and even higher, jagged, snowy, monuments of rock soared into the sky.

Doyle pointed toward one of them, "That was the one we saw that stuck out like a white tooth above the horizon".

"I wouldn't know, I had my hands over my eyes but I suppose you didn't notice".

"You mean I noticed distant Himalayan peaks but failed to notice the person next to me," said Doyle, laughing at himself, until he realised Doyle wasn't amused, "Oh, I'm sorry, I didn't mean to…".

Shona managed a nod and a very slight smile.

In the alleyways of Namche, light filtered down over a dark ridgeline. A snow-covered face striped with bands of rock, reared high above the ridge.

"We have to climb up that ridge somewhere, tomorrow," announced Doyle.

"You don't mean we are going up something as steep as that!" squealed Shona. If Doyle's plan was to share a serene, gentle time to calm their marriage, it certainly wasn't succeeding.

Shona marched off toward Namche market, where she came across a startling array of bright, beautifully patterned hats, bags, scarfs, beads, bracelets and bell sashes. Doyle followed but veered away to where ponies were being walked bare-back past people wearing colourful jackets, along alleyways of brown dirt, below blue roofs.

Shona was looking for a brightly coloured headscarf to keep her warm. As Doyle approached, he had the sensitivity to notice which one had caught her eye, and promptly bought the headscarf.

"It's funny," said Shona, semi-serious but laughing now. "When the plane came down to land at Lukla, we nearly had a divorce on our hands".

"You're right," said Doyle, "You must have wondered whether I'd come here to see the mountains or to spend time with you".

"But, this is your chance," said Shona, with an upbeat voice, "I've given up a great time with Beth and Luke, in order to come on this adventure with you".

"Hope you think it's worth it. What was the best thing you did today?" asked Doyle.

"Well, it wasn't the helicopter ride".

In the morning, waking up in the Himalayas was as beautiful as it was difficult for Shona. Already, at breakfast she had a headache and was feeling sick. Was it altitude sickness?

"Perhaps we should stay here," said Doyle.

"No, I wouldn't miss the trek for the world," said Shona, bravely.

"Are you sure?"

Coming out of Namche Bazaar, the slope was so steep that Shona had to stop for a rest every ten or fifteen steps. The headache was still throbbing, but Shona wouldn't turn back. Doyle stood supportively at her side, at each resting place.

"You know, you really don't have to do this," he said.

"Yes, I do. I want to enjoy what you enjoy," she said, and looking down at Namche Bazaar huddled below, she whispered to herself, "and I don't want to be ruled by fear".

"The slope gets much easier in a little while," said Doyle, looking up, not realizing just how much that news soothed Shona.

After the break of slope above, Shona was comfortable with the walking, and her headache left her. They reached the hotel high on the ridge and stood by the outdoor tables to look at the view.

"It's good of them to allow us here," said Doyle as they sat down to eat. "They let us sit at the tables even though we're not staying at the hotel".

"Well, it's not like your average hotel," said Shona, looking round at the breath-taking vista, high above the world.

"Let's go and see what we can see," said Doyle, nodding toward the stone wall at the edge of the Everest View hotel grounds.

Doyle knelt down by the wall, "I've been so unreasonable," he said, producing a bead necklace from his pocket. "Would you forgive me?"

"You've brought me here to say that?"

"Yes," he said, placing the necklace he'd secretly bought in Namche Bazaar, over her head.

They both looked at the mountains.

"What's the name of that beautiful-looking mountain?" she asked.

"It's Ama Dablam. Look, that's Everest over there".

"Where?" she laughed.

"Can you see that high ridge," he said, pointing. "It runs to an end at a mountain called Lhotse".

"Yes".

"Mount Everest stands above and behind the ridge, just before Lhotse".

"Yes, I can see it now".

"Between the ridge and Everest is the Khumbu icefall. The first ascent of Everest went up that way", said Doyle, staring into the distance.

The left side of Everest was bathed in blue sky, but to its right, mist was steaming off the mountain, spinning into long cloud drifts stretching out along the direction of the wind raking across its summit.

"You know, when you knelt down I thought you were praying," beamed Shona.

"No, I've thought about it, especially in places like this" he admitted. "When you go to church, I sometimes wonder about God," he said, turning round to look again at Ama Dablam and Everest, "but this is my church, these mountains. This is what I find awesome".

Shona wanted to say that mountains have no compassion, they're just there, but she said nothing. Instead, it was a special moment, as together they soaked in the view. On the way down, they stood on a rock that straddled the path, completely taken by the sight of the snow-clothed, stone monoliths shimmering in the distance.

·········●··········

Down in Kathmandu, as evening fell, children were playing outside. Luke, Beth and Aashish had joined a dozen or so, aged anything between four and fourteen, playing in an open area, shaded by trees.

All of a sudden, the children ran to collect sticks and Beth looked at Luke in alarm as they returned with a stick in each hand. "Not to worry," said Aashish. "They're going to do juggling".

Whilst some started to juggle, others were holding a stick out and balancing another at its midpoint at right angles to it, for as long as they could.

Then, one by one, the children began to stop what they were doing and drop their sticks to watch two boys who were trying to outdo one another in batting a stick continuously into the air. They were using a stick to hit another stick upwards a few feet, again and again, tapping the stick under one side then under the other, to keep it balanced in perpetual motion.

The boys battled it out for nearly ten minutes until one outlasted the other. The little crowd gathered around him. "It's your choice what to do next!"

"Ekkhuti!" he shouted.

Aashish leaned toward Beth and Luke. "This is a game we can join in with," he told them. "They're going to use sticks to draw on the ground first".

To Beth and Luke's surprise, instead of drawing pictures in the bare earth as they had expected, the children marked out a huge grid made up of squares big enough for two people to stand in, before they gathered around the outside of the grid. The children then looked at Beth and Luke and nodded to Aashish to ask them to start off what looked like an exciting game.

· · · · · · · ● · · · · · · · · · ·

Amisha, Dhonu, Aashish, Beth and Luke were all waiting, as the plane landed at Katmandhu airport.

Shona was humming and singing as she came down from the aeroplane.

"Is that because you're glad the flight's finished?" asked Doyle.

"No, it's because being in the mountains with you, blew away the cobwebs".

Beth and Luke rushed forward and huddled round them.

"How have they been?" asked Doyle, as Amisha and Dhonu came up to greet them.

"We've hardly seen them," Amisha replied. "How was your time in the mountains?"

"It just made me want to sing".

"Auntie Shona plays the guitar and sings for us," said Beth.

"Rather well," agreed Dhonu, as they walked toward the car. "We've heard her too".

"Have you brought your guitar?" asked Amisha.

"No".

"Sing for us on the way home, Auntie Shona," pleaded Beth.

"To be sure, you've a lovely voice!" urged Doyle.

"Go on, Aunt Shona, please sing for us what you were singing," called Luke.

All went quiet. Shona looked out at the runway as the plane they'd arrived in taxied into the distance. Beyond the buildings, the high peaks of the Ganesh Himal range soared into a blue sky. She stood still. "Do you really want me to sing the song I was singing?"

"We do," cried Beth, speaking for Luke as well.

It was then that Shona remembered the blue, sparkling sky on a different day above a Sierra mountain called Sky, and the cross that stands on its summit. She searched her mind, and said, "You might think the song is about something too rugged to sing about, but I sing because of the passion of Jesus, my Saviour, that he died on a cursed tree, and that they laid his body down in a tomb, with many tears, and sealed the entrance with a heavy stone…".

"Your song is about our clues," interrupted Beth. "Did you know that?"

"No, I did not"

"Was there an ancient curse on the 'tree'?" asked Luke.

"Not really, I suppose. The song is about Jesus, who took away the curse of sin so that we could be forgiven" answered Shona.

"Do you mind us telling you about what we discovered from the clues in our dream?" asked Luke, politely.

"Not at all," Shona replied. "Go ahead, but let's climb into the van first".

"BC was over," he began, standing in the car park, "and the ancient world came to an end with Jesus".

"Yes," replied Shona, opening the van door.

Everyone climbed in and slid the doors closed and waited for someone to speak.

"Jesus told his followers about the beautiful things that are blessed in people," said Beth, as she looked through the window at the mountains.

"And he said to bless and not curse," added Luke, "not even your enemies".

Beth leant forward and asked, "How can you love and bless someone who has done you wrong?"

"It has to start somewhere," Shona sighed. "I can't understand just how it can be, but God so loved the world that He gave His only Son, destroying the power of the curse on the cross, making it a tree of life so that whoever believes on Him should not perish but have everlasting life".

"And the 'heavy stone' in your song was rolled away," said Luke, "and Jesus came back to life".

"He did. The women saw him first," said Amisha. "When he appeared to the disciples, they thought they'd seen a ghost, but then he asked them for something to eat. He even cooked them fish for breakfast!"

"Have you enjoyed the Nepalese food?" asked Doyle, changing the subject.

"Yes," chimed Beth and Luke.

"What have you been doing with yourselves?" asked Shona.

"Playing games," answered Beth.

"What sort of games?"

"Games with sticks that need hard skills," said Luke.

"Not all of them," said Beth, "for one game we used sticks to draw a grid on the ground and take turns hopping from square to square".

"The skill there is to land on the square with a stone in, and kick it at the same time," said Luke. "The first one to go all the way round throws the stone over a shoulder, and it lands in another square".

"I played games with sticks that needed hard skills when I was studying in England," said Dhonu.

"Did you?" asked Shona, wondering what he meant.

"Yes, games with wickets" laughed Dhonu, "called cricket!"

The sunset over Kathmandu looked like fiery, crackling balls of explosions, pierced through by shafts and corridors of light. Dark black wisps and white puffs of cloud hovered in front of cloud banks blazing pink with the last of the day.

12

DREAMS OF GRACE

Beads of perspiration dotted Beth's forehead and Luke's hair was almost wet through, as they stood at the door, having arrived back from the centre of Kathmandu.

"What have you been doing there…having a sauna?" asked Doyle.

"There were so many indoor shopping centres, we got lost in them," moaned Beth.

"I told you it would be better to wait and go with Aashish," said Shona.

"Yes, but one of the presents was for Aashish. We didn't want him to see it," said Luke, looking around. "Where is he?"

"He's in the van, waiting for you".

Luke and Beth left the presents in the house and squeezed into the van with Aashish, next to the food boxes stashed on the back seat, with Doyle on the other side.

"Why are you so late?" asked Aashish.

"To be honest," said Beth, "Luke made a friend and when he got off, Luke gave him the thumbs-up and said goodbye through the bus window, but the guard came and threw Luke off the bus. So I had to get out and run home with him".

Aashish winced, "Thumb-up is the sign to tell the guard you want to get off the bus and go to the toilet". As it sank in, they collapsed into fits of laughter.

The van set off with a jolt. In front of them, Amisha was telling Shona about women running goat farming businesses, and Dhonu was explaining to Doyle behind him, how churches were being made more child-friendly.

"Dreams can come true, with support from people like you," said Dhonu. "Today, we hope you will see what a difference it makes".

Ten minutes later the car was moving slowly in traffic, and Beth found herself gazing up at an ornately carved wooden verandah. Below it, she caught sight of neatly folded piles of colourful textiles laid out on the ground.

Noticing that she was interested in them, Aashish leaned in front of Luke, who was in between, and said, "They're saris. They make them here, and they make carpets too".

Seconds later, the van lurched to a stop and a couple of food boxes next to them fell into the footwell. Aashish picked them up and as he placed them carefully back on the seat, Dhonu turned round, leaning his arm against the top of his seat,

"Yes, this is where the factories are that we raided," he declared.

Luke's ears perked up, "You raided factories?" He was wondering which side of the law today's mission was.

"To be precise, we raided thirty nine sari factories".

"What for?" asked Beth, wondering if the police had caught up with him yet.

"To find children at risk and set them free".

As soon as Dhonu saw the mixture of relief and concern on Luke and Beth's faces, he said, "Don't worry, government agencies were working with us".

As they stepped out of the van to have a look around, Luke felt a bit like a government agent on an inspection.

Beth ran to look at the saris. "They're lovely. Why did the children need to be rescued?"

"You should ask them," replied Amisha. "They were made to work very long hours".

"But an hour only lasts an hour," said Beth. "You can't have a very long hour".

"Beth, don't be so literal," yelled Luke, immediately regretting his tone. "Please go on, Amisha, she's like this sometimes, but she doesn't mean any harm".

"Let's put it this way," said Amisha, gently, "having worked all day, if children were sleepy after dinner at 8 o' clock, they would be beaten, punished and assaulted until they continued to do the work that was required".

An auto rickshaw passed by a little too close for comfort, so Amisha pointed across the road, "Let's go somewhere quieter".

There, on the other side of the road, was a tea and curd shop and somewhere to buy a drink and sit down.

A busy waiter was moving so quickly around the room with plates wobbling on his arm, that Beth said, "If he takes one slightly wrong step, there'll be a terrible accident".

"That's how it works round here. People are working overtime trying to do as much as possible in a day," sighed Amisha.

"Would you believe that little kids have been working in the factories from 7am to midnight?" Dhonu's eyes shone with a sense of outrage. "They were mistreated. Some children's hands were broken by the punishments and many children had scars all over their bodies".

Beth's eyes glistened, "I'm very sorry to hear that," she said.

Returning to the van, Doyle stopped and took a good look around. He grunted, "Anyone overworking is in danger of missing out on life's opportunities".

"Well, you're not in any danger of that!" laughed Shona, "I think the point is that these children had no choice".

"Yeah, well maybe there's a lesson there for me," Doyle looked down, and noticed some carpets piled on the ground nearby.

"So, are you out of work at the moment, Doyle?" asked Dhonu.

"I am. I was working at a chocolate factory, then one day they pulled the rug from under us. There was nothing I could do about it," he looked at the people passing by and going about their business. "At least, by working hard, people here can hold on to work".

"Yes, but being exploited in forced labour, is something else," said Dhonu. "Children as young as six, were being trapped all day long in these sari factories".

"How do you mean, 'trapped'?" asked Shona, after they'd climbed into the van.

"Working more than twelve hours a day, with no education," groaned Amisha, "the door was closed on their future".

"That's like a doom stone," said Luke, suddenly realizing that no-one around him, apart from Beth, knew what he was talking about. "You know, we found a cave in the cliffs, a place of fear for the village below, because a large stone blocked most of the cave entrance, and if anyone went into the cave and people wanted to be unkind to them and push the stone across the gap, they were doomed".

"The children in the embroidered sari factories, were doomed to forced labour," said Dhonu, "as long as no-one did anything about it".

"But you changed that," said Shona.

"Not just us," said Dhonu, as the van accelerated. "Our Nepal network to help children was given responsibility to act by the police. We were helped by church volunteers and people from the community".

"And how many children did you rescue?"

"Nearly two hundred," said Dhonu, "and we moved them into transit shelters, looked after their nutrition and health care, and let them speak and listen to trained counsellors. After a week or so, we re-united as many as we could with their families. We had eighty volunteers from different churches in Kathmandu helping us free the children and get them looked after".

"It sounds like a dream come true," mused Doyle.

"We have many dreams and we pray them to a God who listens," said Amisha. "All we needed to be was willing and God gave us favour with the government and the police, and the grace to do it".

"It's God in action," said Dhonu. "It's only a fraction of what He's given us to do. We've been working with a charity in Oxford, England, that cares for abandoned and abused children and works with partner networks like us all round the world".

"It must be so worthwhile," said Doyle, "to help make such a difference in the lives of children. I wish I could help to do that".

"What's the name of the charity you work with in England?" asked Shona.

"*Viva*, it means live long," answered Amisha. "And what have you learned from your clues, Beth and Luke?"

"That the cycle of doom can be broken when someone does something about it," said Luke.

"And that we live in an age when we can do something about it," said Beth, "but it all seems like a dream".

"I think you've been dreaming about what it means to be living in the age of grace," said Shona.

"I can't wait to tell everyone at home about all this!" roared Luke.

"Do you think we'll have another dream?" wondered Beth.

"You can dream for me that I'll find some work to do!" said Doyle.

ABOUT VIVA

The story about the children rescued from sari factories in Nepal in Chapter 12 is based on true events. In September 2012, Viva's partner network CarNet Nepal reunited 124 trafficked children with their families after they were rescued from the squalid conditions of the embroidery factories in which they had been forced to live and work.

I first came across the work of Viva and their partner networks in 2007, when my daughter Jo started to work for them.

Viva is an international children's charity passionate about releasing children from poverty and abuse. They grow locally-led networks committed to working together so that children are safe, well and able to fulfil their God-given potential. To find out more about their work, visit Viva's website – www.viva.org

Printed in the United States
By Bookmasters